THE RINGMASTER'S SECRET

Nancy is given a beautiful gold bracelet and finds that one of the horse charms is missing. When she learns the unusual story behind the jewelry, she sets out to solve the fascinating mystery.

The bracelet had been presented to a former circus performer by a queen who loved horses. For some reason the performer had to sell the bracelet but would not reveal her true identity.

Clues lead Nancy to Sims' Circus, where she meets Lolita, an unhappy young aerialist who has a horse charm wrought exactly like those on Nancy's bracelet. The young detective joins the circus and is soon caught up in its exciting life. It becomes apparent that someone opposes Nancy's investigation and tries to deter her.

Nancy's clever deductions help her to find the original owner of the bracelet, to reunite a mother and daughter who had been separated for years, and to bring much happiness to Sims' Circus.

"Now we can get out of this prison," George cried.

NANCY DREW MYSTERY STORIES

The Ringmaster's Secret

BY CAROLYN KEENE

PUBLISHERS   *Grosset & Dunlap*   NEW YORK

Contents

The
Ringmaster's Secret

CHAPTER I

The Golden Charms

"Oh, Nancy, I worry so about your doing that trick riding," remarked Hannah Gruen, looking fondly at the slender attractive girl in jodhpurs and a tight-fitting coat.

Eighteen-year-old Nancy Drew was about to leave the house for a morning riding lesson. She had paused to look at the mail on the front-hall table.

"Who knows, Hannah, the trick riding may come in handy someday when I have a mystery to solve," she replied, putting an arm affectionately around the Drews' housekeeper. The kindly middle-aged woman had acted as a mother to her since Mrs. Drew's death many years before.

Nancy added with a smile, "If you're worrying about my safety, I haven't had a spill in months. Señor Roberto is too good a teach—why,

1

look!" she interrupted herself. "Here's a letter and the mystery package from New York!"

"What do you mean, Nancy?"

"Didn't I tell you, Hannah? Aunt Eloise sent a card saying she was mailing me a gift that has an unusual story."

Nancy opened the letter from her aunt and began to read part of it aloud:

> . . . and the shopkeeper, who purchased it on a buying trip in Europe, said it had been presented to a woman circus performer by a queen who loved horses. The performer was in dire need of money and had to sell it but would not reveal her true identity. . . .

As Nancy paused, Hannah Gruen remarked with a sigh, "And I suppose that you're going to try to find this circus performer and help her out of her troubles. That's what you always do. Well, open the box and let's see what the mysterious gift is."

Nancy unwrapped several layers of tissue paper before she came to Aunt Eloise's present. Then, holding up an exquisite gold bracelet, she exclaimed, "Look at all those darling little horse charms on it! One, two, three, four, five of them! Oh, oh, a sixth one is missing."

"It doesn't matter," said Hannah. "The bracelet's beautiful enough without the other horse."

"Yes, it's perfectly lovely."

"Oh, oh, a sixth charm is missing!"

Nancy slipped the dainty bracelet over her wrist and held up her arm to look at the effect. The tiny horses gleamed in the light and seemed to be almost alive, they were so perfectly wrought. Each displayed a different gait, and all were gracefully poised.

"I wonder which gait the sixth horse had," Nancy mused.

"There are only five gaits, aren't there?" Mrs. Gruen asked.

"Yes. It's possible the missing figure wasn't a horse at all," Nancy said.

Turning the bracelet around and around, she continued to admire it and to scrutinize the jewelry thoroughly for any sign of the original owner—the person who would not, according to the story, reveal her identity. There were no initials on the bracelet, and the simple scroll design on the wristlet did not seem to hold the answer.

"Do you suppose the circus performer was a European?" Nancy asked, "or an American who was working over there?"

"Now, Nancy," said Mrs. Gruen, "you know I wouldn't have the least idea."

The girl's blue eyes suddenly sparkled and she snapped her fingers. "I can start checking right away by asking Señor Roberto some questions. You know, he used to be with the Sims Circus."

"Yes, and I wish he'd never left it and opened

that riding academy here in River Heights," Hannah declared. "Then you wouldn't have learned how to ride without a saddle and jump onto a moving horse and——"

Nancy laughed. "It's fun. And by the way, did you know the Sims Circus is coming to town tomorrow?"

"You bet it is," said a young voice from the back of the hall.

Nancy and Hannah turned to see six-year-old Teddy Brown, a neighbor, who had come in the back entrance. The red-haired, freckle-faced boy was grinning broadly.

"And don't forget, Nancy," he went on, "you promised to take me to see the circus men put up the tents and everything."

"That's right, Teddy. We'll leave your house at five o'clock tomorrow morning." Nancy tweaked his nose affectionately. "That's very early. Sure you'll be up?"

"You bet! I'll be seeing you at five tomorrow morning."

The youngster ran off as quickly as he had appeared. As the back screen-door slammed behind him, Nancy removed the bracelet and handed it to Hannah Gruen.

"Please put this away for me," she requested. "I won't be gone long."

"And promise me you'll be careful," the housekeeper pleaded. "I wouldn't want your father to come home from his trip and find that you——"

"Don't say it, Hannah!"

Nancy kissed her and promised to be careful. Seated in her convertible, her reddish-blond hair blowing in the soft summer breeze as she drove along, Nancy made a charming picture. But her expression was serious and her thoughts were on the circus performer. The young detective wondered what misfortune the woman had met.

Ten minutes later Nancy parked the car in the driveway of the riding academy and walked to Señor Roberto's office. Hitch, the stableman, greeted her with his usual glum manner. The groom, whom Nancy knew only by his nickname, never changed his dour expression.

"The boss ain't here," he muttered. He suddenly shook his finger at Nancy. "If you know what's good for you, Miss Drew, you'll stay away from circus ridin'."

"Circus riding?" Nancy asked, puzzled. "I haven't been doing any circus riding."

"Yes, you have too." Hitch's voice was rising angrily. "That's what Roberto tries on everybody who shows a leanin' for it. But I'm tellin' you, quit it! Stop now! Right now!"

Nancy stared in amazement at Hitch, whose eyes were blazing. What could be back of his outburst, she wondered. A hatred of Roberto?

"Nobody what ain't been brought up in a circus

has got any right to try imitatin' circus folks!"
Hitch shouted. "I tell you——"

The tirade ended abruptly when the stableman saw Señor Roberto walking across the outdoor riding ring toward his office. The irate helper ambled off, saying he would bring Nancy's mare. She stepped outside.

"Good afternoon, Miss Drew," the riding master said with a smile. "Sorry to be late."

"I didn't mind waiting," Nancy replied. "Hitch and I were talking. He—er—seemed a bit upset."

"About the circus, no doubt," Roberto commented. "Hitch will never get over his dismissal from Sims'. He doesn't talk about much else."

"I presume he's rather keyed up because the circus is coming here tomorrow," Nancy remarked.

"To tell you the truth, Miss Drew, Hitch is beside himself. He has declared he won't go near it, but I wonder if he can resist. Anyway, I'm going. I want to see what acts they have now and say hello to my old friends."

As Roberto finished speaking, Hitch led Nancy's mare into the ring. The beautiful gray horse nuzzled the girl as she stroked the animal's velvety nose. Nancy swung into the saddle and walked her horse counterclockwise several times around the ring.

Then Señor Roberto called out, "Trot!"

Nancy automatically sat still for a few strides, then started posting, remembering to take the up motion when the mare's left foreleg was forward in order to get the correct diagonal. The riding master smiled in satisfaction at the rhythm and grace of Nancy's performance.

Next came the canter. Half an hour later, Nancy was ready for stunt riding. First Hitch removed the saddle, looking darkly at Nancy as he carried it away.

Once more she mounted the horse, this time with only the blanket between herself and the mare. Nancy slapped her gently on the flank and the horse began to canter slowly. Being an ex-circus horse, Belgian Star was considerate of her rider.

She seemed to know just the right speed to use, too, as Nancy stood up on the mare's back. Keeping her balance, Nancy went twice around the enclosure. On the third lap she caught a fleeting glimpse of a figure crouching on the ground outside the split-rail fence.

The next moment, a large stone sailed through the air directly at Belgian Star's head. The horse reared almost straight up, and Nancy was thrown off.

CHAPTER II

A Suspicious Groom

ON THE far side of the ring Señor Roberto had witnessed the accident in alarm and dismay. He rushed toward Nancy, who lay still on the turf where she had fallen. As he reached her, the girl's eyelids flickered open.

"Miss Drew!" the riding master cried.

He kneeled beside her, hoping that she had broken no bones and had not hit her head.

"Miss Drew!" he murmured over and over. "Are you all right?"

Nancy nodded slowly and struggled to a sitting position. Then, with Señor Roberto's assistance, she got to her feet. To the man's amazement, her first words were, "Is Belgian Star all right?"

It was typical of Nancy not to think of herself. She had been in many tight spots while solving the various mysteries that had come her way, but the safety of innocent persons involved had always been her chief concern. Starting with *The Secret of the Old Clock*, she had proved herself adept in handling difficult situations and bringing many criminals to justice. This had been particularly true in her most recent case, which had come to be known as *The Clue of The Velvet Mask*.

"Miss Drew," said Señor Roberto, "you look very pale. We'll go into my office and I'll fix you some tea."

Nancy was not to be sidetracked in her concern for Belgian Star. The horse had left the ring and was now out of sight.

"Where did Star go?" she asked. "Is she all right?"

"Well," said Señor Roberto, raising his eyebrows high, "my first concern is for you. But if you insist upon knowing about the horse, I'll find out."

Nancy managed a wan smile. "I didn't mean to seem ungrateful," she said, "but someone hurled a stone at Star's head. It may have injured her."

The riding master stared in amazement. "You say someone threw a stone at the horse?" he asked.

Nancy nodded. "A man who was lying on the ground outside the fence tossed it. There's the stone over on the grass." She pointed.

Señor Roberto looked worried. "I understand now why you were anxious about the mare," he said. "We'll look into this at once. Have you any idea who the person was?"

"No, I haven't," Nancy replied. "I didn't see his face."

Suddenly the riding master bellowed, "Hitch! Hitch! Come here at once!"

The stableman did not appear instantly. But after the third summons he ran from the building.

"Were you out here when Miss Drew fell?" the riding master asked him.

"Why, no, sir," the groom replied. "I didn't even know there'd been any trouble."

"Did you see anyone outside the fence?"

"No, sir."

"Did Belgian Star run into her stall?" Roberto questioned him.

"Yes, she did. Star seemed pretty excited. I've been tryin' to calm her down."

While the riding master told his hostler about the accident, Nancy noticed that Hitch was wearing the same kind of clothes and old soft hat as the figure she had seen on the ground. And his suit had fresh dirt on it! Her suspicions were instantly aroused. She looked beyond the fence to determine whether the man might have had time to take a circuitous route back to the stable.

"He could have done it easily," she told herself, staring at the thick woods that came up almost to the fence of the riding ring. "And Hitch is out of breath from running."

Nancy turned to Señor Roberto, "How long was I unconscious?" she asked.

"Oh, twenty or thirty seconds—that's all," the riding master replied.

Then Nancy turned to Hitch. "How did you get all that fresh dirt on the front of your clothes?"

Hitch suddenly looked uncomfortable. He did not reply for a few seconds. Instead he countered, "I've heard you're a detective. Is it true?"

Nancy, somewhat taken aback by his question, acknowledged that she was known as an amateur sleuth.

"Then I guess I'd better tell the truth—seein' as how you'll find it out in the end," Hitch said. "I walked around through the woods to watch you do the circus stunts. While I was lookin', I seen a feller lyin' on the ground by the fence. The next thing I knew he threw somethin' at your horse. Then when I seen you fall off I got so scared I beat it. That's when I tripped and fell down in the dirt."

"Have you any idea who the man was?" Señor Roberto inquired in a cold voice.

Hitch said he had not seen the man's face and was sorry now he had not waited to find out.

"I'm mighty glad you're all right, Miss Drew," he added, and then he walked back to the stable.

There was nothing more Nancy could do. Despite the groom's story, she felt sure he had thrown the stone. But why had he tried to harm her and Belgian Star?

"I'll watch him from now on," Nancy decided.

She told Señor Roberto that she felt fully recovered from her spill, and if Belgian Star was
all right, she wanted to continue her riding
lesson.

The riding master was about to demur, then
changed his mind. He believed a rider who had
fallen off should immediately remount his horse
if he had not been injured.

Hitch brought Belgian Star from the stable.
Nancy and the riding master carefully examined
the mare's nose, and though there was a bruise on
it, the horse did not seem to be suffering any
pain.

"Are you game to go on with your lesson?"
Nancy asked the mare, putting her arms around
the animal's gracefully arched neck.

For answer, Belgian Star went into the ring
and waited for Nancy to mount. This time the
girl circled the enclosure several times before
attempting to stand up on the horse's back.

"Am I imagining it, or is someone peering at
me from among those trees?" she asked herself,
trying to shrug off a distrustful mood.

As she rounded the curve on the next lap,
Nancy was sure she was not wrong—someone *was*
watching. A feeling of uneasiness came over her.

She had just about decided to practice stunt
riding when she heard a voice call her. She turned
abruptly to see two girls running from the woods.
They climbed onto the fence, laughing.

"Bess! George!" Nancy cried. "Where did you come from?"

She immediately rode Belgian Star over to them. She noticed that blond, blue-eyed and slightly plump Bess Marvin had a sketching pad and pencil in her hands.

"Hold it!" Bess ordered.

Nancy obediently sat still while her friend quickly sketched. Meanwhile, Bess's cousin, George Fayne, leaned over the fence and patted Belgian Star. She was slim and athletic looking. Her dark-brown hair was cut very short.

"Pretty nice horse," she remarked. "Is your dad going to let you buy her?"

"Oh, Señor Roberto wouldn't part with this mare for anything," Nancy replied. "She's a darling. I wouldn't ride any other horse out here."

"Let's see you do some stunts," George urged.

"Yes, please do," said Bess. "I want to make several sketches."

"All right," Nancy agreed. "But, Bess, first tell me, when did you take up sketching?"

"Just this afternoon." Bess giggled. "You might say I was inspired by reports of your fine riding."

Nancy told the girls what had happened to her a short time before and asked if they had seen a man running as they came through the woods. Neither of them had, but George offered to stand guard while Nancy did her trick riding.

Bess and George were amazed at their friend's

proficiency as an equestrienne. Nancy somersaulted from Belgian Star to the ground and then
leaped onto the mare's back as the horse cantered
around the ring.

"You're a whiz!" George said admiringly. "And
you sure kept all this a secret."

"How did you find out about my taking these
lessons?" Nancy asked as the girls walked toward
the stable.

"From Hannah Gruen," George replied. "She's
worried about you and this trick riding, Nancy."

"I know Hannah is concerned," the pretty
sleuth answered. "But I've promised not to break
any bones."

Nancy introduced her friends to Señor Roberto.
Then she told them about the bracelet she had
received from Aunt Eloise. She asked the riding
master if he had ever seen or heard about a horse-
charm bracelet that had been presented to a circus
performer by a queen.

"Why do you ask?" Señor Roberto wrinkled
his brow as if trying to remember something.

Nancy related the story connected with the
bracelet. Then Señor Roberto said he had heard
such a tale but could not recall who had told it.

"I seem to remember, though," he added
slowly, "that the story involved a strange disap-
pearance. Whether it was the bracelet or the
owner or the giver, I don't know."

He called Hitch and asked him whether he had

ever heard about a horse-charm bracelet. The riding master briefly repeated the story Nancy had told him. The stableman looked first at Nancy and then at his employer.

Finally, in a gruff tone, he replied, "Yes, I heard about a bracelet like that pony one when I was workin' for Sims' Circus."

"Do you remember who told you?" Nancy asked.

The groom thought for several seconds, then said he could not recall. Shrugging, he added, "You know how it is in the circus. All kinds o' stories get around."

Although Nancy was disappointed not to learn more, she hoped to be able to question members of Sims' Circus the next day. By the following evening she might know the history of the bracelet.

For this reason getting up at four thirty the next morning did not seem like such a chore. Teddy was sitting on the doorstep when Nancy arrived at the Browns'. The two set off for the circus grounds in Nancy's convertible.

It seemed as if all the children in River Heights had gathered to watch the big tents being put up. Boys and girls were running in every direction in order not to miss anything. The good-natured workmen did not seem to mind the excitement and confusion.

Nancy had a hard time keeping track of Teddy.

For a while she held onto his hand, running along with him as he darted from place to place.

A short respite came as he paused to watch the elephants being watered in a large tent. It was a thrill for the small boy when a man handed him a bucket and asked if he would like to let Old Jumbo, the biggest elephant, drink out of it.

"Can I really!" Teddy asked gleefully.

Just then a girl's voice called, "Hi, Nancy!"

It was George. She had her little neighbor in tow. The two girls chatted for a few seconds; then Nancy turned back to watch Teddy. He was not in sight!

"Oh, my goodness!" Nancy said, worried. "I thought he was giving the elephant a drink."

She looked around the tent. Not seeing Teddy there, Nancy dashed outside. Her eyes scanned the crowd. Finally she spotted the red-haired boy and hurried toward him.

But before she could reach him, Nancy was horror-struck to see a large pole on a truck next to the boy begin to slide. If he did not get out of the way, it would strike him!

"Teddy!" Nancy screamed. "Run!"

CHAPTER III

The Cruel Ringmaster

THE little boy looked puzzled by Nancy's cry. For a harrowing second she thought he would not obey. But he jumped out of the way in the nick of time. The pole landed on the ground with a tremendous crash.

Nancy dashed up to the boy and threw her arms around him. Her heart was pounding wildly. "Oh, Teddy," she cried, "you gave me such a fright!"

"I'm sorry, Nancy," the little boy said. "I won't leave you again."

Nancy and Teddy walked about, enjoying the excitement. They paused to look at a long row of portable stoves on which the circus chefs were cooking breakfast.

"Mm!" Teddy exclaimed. "That smells good!"

At that moment a man brushed rudely by them, pushing the little boy out of his way. The man

18

was tall and wore a long mustache. His black hair stood straight up, and his eyes flashed. On one arm was a large tattoo.

"Is he one of the freaks?" Teddy asked loudly enough for the man to hear. The little boy had never seen a tattoo.

The man stopped short. He turned and glared at Teddy. Then, pointing a menacing finger, he exclaimed, "Get out of here!"

Teddy clung to Nancy, who tried to apologize for the boy.

The man would not listen. "I said, get out of here!" he repeated. "Visitors aren't supposed to be near the cafeteria."

As Nancy led Teddy away, a pleasant-looking woman carrying costumes over her arm passed by. Nancy stopped her and asked about the man with the mustache.

"That's our ringmaster. His name is Reinhold Kroon."

"You mean he snaps the whip and makes the horses go around?" Teddy asked, his eyes wide with interest.

"He does more than that," the woman replied. "He announces all the acts. He used to be a horseman, but he's practically in charge of the whole circus now."

Nancy asked the woman whether she had ever known anyone in the circus who owned a horse-charm bracelet.

"No, I haven't," she replied. "Does it have something to do with this circus?"

"It might," Nancy replied. "Where can I find Mr. Sims?"

The woman said that Mr. Sims rarely traveled with the circus. Mr. Kroon was apparently in charge now. She suggested that Nancy ask him about the bracelet.

Since the ringmaster had not seemed to be in the mood to answer questions, Nancy decided to wait for another opportunity. She thanked the woman for her information, then she and Teddy walked away.

"We'll go home and have breakfast," Nancy said to the boy. "I'll pick you up at nine o'clock and we'll go watch the parade."

"That'll be great," Teddy agreed.

Hannah Gruen was preparing breakfast when Nancy reached home and asked whether Mr. Drew had returned from a business trip.

The housekeeper shook her head. "Your father did telephone, though. He said he didn't know just when he'd be home."

Nancy looked wistful. She missed her father when his legal work took him out of town. She enjoyed discussing his cases with him and also getting his advice on any mysteries she might be working on.

"Breakfast is ready," Mrs. Gruen announced.

"Did you find out anything about your bracelet at the circus?"

"No, but I'll talk to more of the people. The circus will be here for two or three days."

At nine o'clock Nancy and Teddy were on their way to the main street of River Heights along which the circus parade would come. The street was already lined with people, and they had to walk several blocks before they found a place at the curb.

A few minutes later they heard a band. The music grew louder and louder, and the marching players came into view. Teddy clapped his hands and jumped up and down.

"Here come the elephants," Nancy announced as the enormous animals swung up the street. Men and women attired in gay costumes accompanied the elephants. The men were seated astride the animals' backs, while the girls walked alongside. Occasionally they would seat themselves on the elephants' curled-up trunks and ride for a short distance before jumping off.

"I bet that would be fun," Teddy said. "Here comes Cinderella in a gold carriage."

"She's the main attraction in the circus, I understand," Nancy remarked. "Her name is Lolita. She does a very daring trapeze act."

As the carriage glided by, drawn by four beautiful white horses, Lolita waved to the people, who clapped their hands and shouted. But the lovely, dark-haired girl did not smile in return.

"Why is she so sad?" Teddy asked. "She looks like Cinderella did after her coach turned into a pumpkin."

"I wonder too," Nancy replied.

Just then the parade halted. Without warning Teddy dashed into the street. He ran down to Cinderella's coach. Reaching up, he opened the door and hopped inside.

Nancy was at the boy's heels. No sooner had Teddy seated himself beside Lolita, than Nancy opened the door. "Come out, Teddy," she said.

For the first time Lolita smiled. She put her arm around Teddy and said, "Let him stay. No one has ever done this before. I think it's nice."

Nancy closed the door. "As soon as you want Teddy to leave, don't hesitate to say so. I'll walk along beside the carriage and take him when he gets out."

Teddy looked up into Cinderella's face. "Why do you look so sad?" he asked.

"Well," the girl said, "you've heard how unhappy the real Cinderella was when she lost her prince, haven't you? I guess I'm sad for the same reason."

Teddy, not understanding, turned to watch the people on the sidewalk. When they cheered, he stood up and waved.

Everything went smoothly for about two blocks.

Then Nancy heard the sudden, sharp clop of horses' hoofs behind her. Looking over her shoulder, she saw the ringmaster galloping toward her. Quickly she jumped to the sidewalk to avoid being run down.

"That man's so mean," she told herself, "I don't see how he gets along with anybody."

To her dismay, Kroon stopped at Cinderella's carriage. Reaching inside, he grabbed Teddy up in his arms and planted him firmly in front of him on the horse.

"You crazy kid!" he shouted. "What are you trying to do? Ruin my parade?"

Unceremoniously he lifted Teddy out of the saddle and plunked him down on the curb. Nancy started to tell the irate ringmaster that his actions were quite unwarranted since Lolita had said the child might ride with her, but Kroon rode off in a hurry. There were so many animals and circus people to look at—riders, clowns, giants, and midgets—that Nancy and Teddy soon forgot the unpleasant incident.

Both were eager to attend the afternoon performance and arrived early at the circus grounds. Nancy wore an attractive blue sports dress and had slipped the horse-charm bracelet over her wrist. Bess and George, who had her neighbor's son with her, joined Nancy and Teddy. They had front-row seats in one of the center boxes.

The performance began with a second parade

for the benefit of those who had not seen the one on the street. When it was over, the entrance gate opened and seven clowns came running in. Teddy shrieked in delight.

One clown, dressed as a tattered hobo, had a little fox terrier with him that did tricks. Another clown, in farmer's clothes, was wearing a beard that reached his knees. With it, he tickled the ears of a comical-looking cow, composed of two clowns. The fifth clown represented a barrel and did all sorts of tricks rolling around like one.

The last two were dressed in Pierrot clown suits. One carried a tall ladder. Just before he reached the spot where Nancy and her friends were seated, he planted the ladder upright in the ground and held onto it. The other clown, named Pietro, began to climb up. When he reached the top, the clown below suddenly let go and walked off.

"Oh!" everyone under the tent cried.

To their amazement, the clown on the ladder did not fall. He balanced himself skillfully, swaying back and forth above the green tanbark. As everyone realized that this was an exacting stunt, and not just a clownish act, they clapped loudly.

"It's going to be even harder for him to climb down," George observed in a worried voice.

The audience watched breathlessly as the clown slowly lowered himself without falling. He turned in a complete circle to acknowledge the loud applause.

As he bowed low before Nancy's group, a startled look came over his face. The clown walked forward and stared at Nancy's bracelet.

"Where did you get this, miss?" he asked in a low voice.

Before the girl could reply, a whistle sounded and the band began to play. The clown hurriedly said, "My name is Pietro. I must speak to you after the show. Please meet me beside King Kat's cage."

CHAPTER IV

An Amazing Aerialist

"PIETRO!" Nancy called as the clown moved off. "Please tell me——"

Pietro had no opportunity to answer, for at that moment a whistle summoned all the clowns from the ring.

During the acts that followed, Nancy's thoughts reverted constantly to the clown's request that she meet him at the end of the show. Certainly there *was* some secret about her charm bracelet.

When the time came for Lolita's act, all the lights were dimmed except the floodlights on the center ring. Kroon, wearing striped trousers, a Prince Albert coat, and a high silk hat, walked to the microphone.

"Ladies and gentlemen," he announced, "you are about to witness the world's most daring aerial act! Lolita, our Cinderella, will meet her prince in midair and dance with him. But at the stroke of twelve, this brief romance will end."

As the ringmaster retired, the spotlights picked up a small Cinderella carriage being drawn along the tanbark by two white wooden steeds. In it sat beautiful, fairylike Lolita, dressed in a white silver-spangled robe.

The applause was thunderous as attendants attached the carriage to pulleys and Cinderella was slowly pulled up a slanting wire to the top of the tent. Daintily Lolita stood up, discarded her robe, and stepped out in white satin acrobatic tights to a tiny platform suspended from the ceiling.

At once, additional floodlights showed four young men aerialists, signaling for her attention. Smiling, Lolita waited as they swung toward her in turn. But when each man kneeled on the platform and indicated that he wanted to marry Cinderella, Lolita shook her head and he swung away.

Then, as she looked discouraged, a handsome prince in a gleaming silver costume suddenly appeared in the spotlight beside her.

"Prince Charming!" Bess announced, gazing, enthralled, at the performance. Her friends scarcely heard her. Their eyes were fixed on the acrobatic drama far above them. To the strain of a waltz, Cinderella and the prince danced on the tight rope.

At the end of the number they embraced. Then came the sound of a striking gong. One, two—— The prince held Cinderella close. Three, four—— The girl tried to pull away. The gong continued to strike. Eleven, twelve!

Cinderella swung toward the platform where the carriage had been. But the sides of the gorgeous carriage and the white horses had tumbled into a net below. Instead, a pumpkin drawn by mice remained. In a barely perceptible motion, the aerialist had slipped out of her white satin costume and now stood in ragged black tatters!

"Oh!" shrieked Teddy. "Poor Cinderella! Nancy, what will the prince——" He stopped abruptly.

Lolita, about to climb into the pumpkin, suddenly swayed and lost her footing. She plunged downward toward the net!

There was a momentary hush as the audience wondered if this was part of the act. But as Lolita lay still, cries of alarm arose.

"Oh," murmured Teddy. "Is she——"

"Lolita must have fainted," Nancy told him, hoping it was nothing more serious.

From the shadowy stage entrances rushed many circus people, among them Pietro. Ringmaster Kroon waved them aside. Walking under the net, he hissed at Lolita, loudly enough for Nancy to hear, "Get up and take a bow! You're ruining the show!"

Lolita slowly opened her eyes. Pietro reached up and tenderly patted her cheek.

"Leave her alone! Get out of here!" Kroon thundered at the clown.

Pietro, after a glare at his employer, turned back to the girl. Kroon yanked the clown up by his big ruffled collar and sent him sprawling to the tanbark.

"Stand up!" the harsh manager ordered Lolita. This time the girl obeyed, rising slowly and stepping to the edge of the net, where she was helped down by attendants. Lolita acknowledged the tumultuous applause with bow after bow, then left the tent.

Kroon hurried into the ring. "And so," he said, "Cinderella lost her prince. But only temporarily! If you want to see how he found her by matching the glass slipper she wore, come to this evening's performance. Reserve your seats on the way out."

The last act was a clever bareback-riding performance and then came a final pageant, which included the clowns. As soon as it was over, Nancy asked George to take Teddy home; then she started for King Kat's cage to meet Pietro.

The shaggy lion was stalking back and forth restlessly. "How handsome, but how cruel he looks!" Nancy thought. "Just like the ringmaster."

Pietro, who was waiting for her, motioned Nancy to follow him a short distance away from the cage. The clown seemed almost frightened as he said, "I'll talk fast. Visitors aren't allowed here.

If Kroon saw me talking to you, he might discharge me, and that mustn't happen."

"Can't we go some place where he won't see us?" Nancy asked. She wanted to hear everything the clown might have to tell her.

"No, no," he said quickly. "This is the story. Lolita wears a horse charm on a necklace. It is like those on your bracelet and I noticed one is missing. Lolita once said she thought hers came from another piece of jewelry."

"Oh, I must see the necklace!" Nancy said. "Please take me to Lolita."

The clown shook his head. He said that the aerialist was resting for the evening performance and must not be disturbed.

"I understand," Nancy said. "But please go on with your story."

Pietro said that Lolita was Mr. and Mrs. Kroon's adopted daughter. She had lived with them since she was eight years old.

"Have the Kroons and Lolita always been in the circus?" Nancy asked.

The clown nodded and said that Lolita's own parents had been American trapeze artists known as The Flying Flanders.

"What were their names?" Nancy queried.

"John and Lola Flanders." Pietro went on, "The story is that Lolita's parents were killed while performing their act on an extended tour of

Europe. It was then that the Kroons brought Lolita to the United States."

"Did Lolita's parents teach her to be an aerialist?" Nancy asked.

"Oh yes," Pietro replied, "but after they died she was trained by other artists as well."

"She is an excellent performer," Nancy said.

"Yes," the clown agreed, "but Kroon makes her work too hard. He doesn't care about anything but money."

"He does seem dictatorial," Nancy remarked.

The clown looked at her. "That's putting it mildly. Kroon is cruel, and I don't trust him!"

Nancy wondered why Pietro distrusted his employer, but the young man did not explain. Instead he changed the subject and said, "About the horse charm. The one Lolita wears was given to her by her mother when she was only five years old. That was thirteen years ago. I suppose it's only coincidence that the charm looks like those on your bracelet."

"I'm not so sure of that," Nancy remarked.

Quickly she related what she knew of the charm bracelet's history: that the shopkeeper in New York from whom her Aunt Eloise had bought the jewelry had hinted at a mystery. The original owner, supposedly a circus performer, had sold the bracelet because she needed money.

Pietro stared at Nancy in amazement. "That's

very interesting," he said. "I've suspected for a long time that there's some secret in connection with the Kroons and Lolita. But whenever I suggest this to her, she becomes frightened and asks me not to talk about it."

Suddenly a look of alarm came over Pietro's face. "Here comes Kroon now. Run!" he advised. Like a shot he was off, dodging among the various animal cages and trucks until he was out of sight.

Nancy decided not to avoid the ringmaster. She wanted to find out about Lolita's condition. But she had no opportunity to speak to him. He turned abruptly into a nearby tent.

The young detective wondered whether to question any other circus people about Lolita's real parents. She concluded that it would be better to talk with the girl first.

"I'll attend the evening performance," Nancy decided. "Perhaps I'll have a chance to interview the girl then.

"I have a date with Ned," she reminded herself. "I'm sure he'll be glad to come to the circus."

At eight o'clock Ned Nickerson, Emerson College's star football player, arrived at the Drew home. He was a tall, good-looking athlete. Nancy showed him her gold-horse bracelet and told him of the new mystery. Then she asked him if he would take her to the circus.

"Glad to." He grinned. "But listen here, young lady," Ned said, "don't get yourself so mixed up with clowns and aerialists that you can't even find time to talk to me!"

Nancy laughed, but she knew Ned had good reason to scold her. Many times when they had a date she changed the plans completely and involved him in some mystery she was trying to solve.

"Lolita is the most wonderful aerialist I have ever seen," Nancy remarked as they neared the circus grounds.

"I just can't wait to see her," Ned teased. "I may hire myself out as one of those princes."

Nancy made a face at him as he walked up to the ticket office.

"Two in the front row as near the center as possible," Ned told the ticket seller.

"Sorry, sir," the man replied, "there's not even standing room left."

CHAPTER V

A Strange Attack

NANCY looked pleadingly at the ticket seller. Suddenly she had an idea. "Couldn't we just go in to see the animals and side shows?"

The ticket seller thought a moment. "I guess that wouldn't be against fire rules," he said. He called a guard taking tickets at the gate and told him to admit the young lady and her escort.

Nancy and Ned thanked him and hurried inside. Ned inquired what the next move was to be.

Nancy smiled. "First of all, I want to locate Lolita and have a talk with her."

She walked up to one of the midgets, who had just finished entertaining the crowd with a card trick. "Will you please tell me where Lolita's tent is?" she asked him.

He replied in a high-pitched voice. "I'm not allowed to tell."

Nancy was surprised. She wondered if the little

man was trying to be funny, or if this was really a rule of the circus. She moved on to the fat lady, who was seated on a platform next to the midget and repeated her question.

"Sorry, miss," the four-hundred-pound woman answered, "but we're not allowed to give out any information. Mr. Kroon's orders."

Nancy decided she would have to find Lolita's tent by herself! She left Ned watching the fire-eater and hurried off. Walking to the outer fringe of the tent colony, Nancy saw several trailers. Perhaps Lolita, as a star, lived in one of these!

"I'll just wander around among them and see what I can find out," Nancy decided.

Luck was with her. As she approached the first trailer, Nancy could hear two persons arguing heatedly.

"You'll perform tonight and put on a good act, too!" The harsh voice of the ringmaster came to Nancy's ears.

"But, Father, I don't feel well enough to perform! I'm afraid I'll fall again!" It was the young aerialist speaking.

Then Kroon thundered, "I'll give you exactly fifteen minutes to make up your mind, Lolita! Then I'll be back. You'd better decide to perform, because if you don't I'll fire every friend of yours in this circus!"

With that, he rushed out of the trailer and strode off. His face was livid, and Nancy wondered whether the man could be in his right mind.

When he was out of sight, she went to the door of the trailer and tapped. At first there was no response, then a tearful voice said, "Come!"

Lolita was startled at seeing Nancy in the doorway. But when she realized that Nancy wanted to be friendly, she smiled through her tears.

Nancy held up the beautiful charm bracelet. "Pietro tells me you have a gold charm that matches these little horses," she said. "I just couldn't resist the temptation to come and see if by chance it might be the one that is missing from this bracelet."

Lolita fingered the exquisite little horses. Then, going to a bureau drawer, she brought out a dainty gold chain. Hanging from it was a golden horse. The miniature animal, wrought exactly like those on Nancy's bracelet, was a duplicate of the cantering horse charm.

"Your bracelet may have belonged to my lovely mother," said Lolita sadly. "She died when I was only eight years old, but I remember very well how she looked."

"Perhaps she sold the bracelet," Nancy suggested.

Lolita agreed this was possible, but said it would be difficult to determine this definitely. Whenever she asked Mr. and Mrs. Kroon about her parents, the couple changed the subject, saying they did not like to talk about the Flanders' terrible accident.

Leaning close to Nancy, Lolita whispered, "Sometimes I wonder if it's true that my parents are dead."

"Would you like me to help you find out?" Nancy asked on the spur of the moment.

"Oh, could you?" Lolita exclaimed, giving Nancy an impetuous hug.

Nancy told the girl that she had solved a few mysteries and would be glad to find out what she could. She asked if Lolita could give her any information at all, but the young aerialist shook her head.

"As I told you, my foster parents are very close-mouthed. Sometimes I think there must be a reason why they won't tell me anything."

Suddenly Lolita looked at a clock on the wall. The fifteen minutes were up!

"You'd better go," she said abruptly. "Mr. Kroon will be here any moment and he mustn't see you." Suddenly Lolita put her arms around Nancy again. "I never met you until a few minutes ago," she said, "but already you are my friend. I feel much better. Doing my high-wire act seemed impossible before, but now I'll be able to put on a good show."

As they stepped outside, Lolita asked where Nancy would be sitting and said she would wave to her. Learning that the girl and her escort had been unable to obtain tickets, Lolita declared that she would get two for her. She called to a man who was walking past the trailer.

"Dan," she said, "will you come here, please?"

Lolita introduced him as Dan Webster, one of the horse trainers. Then she laughed, saying she had failed to ask her caller's name. When Nancy told her, Lolita said, "Please get Nancy two of the special seats and bring them back here."

As Dan hurried off, Nancy saw Kroon approaching. Quickly she ducked around the corner.

When Kroon reached the trailer, he glared at Lolita. "Well, what's your answer?" he stormed.

"I feel better, Father. I'll do my act," Lolita said quietly.

The man snorted, took her by the arm, and led her away. "Get into your costume," he ordered.

A few minutes later, Dan Webster returned with the tickets. He walked with Nancy as far as the side shows. On the way she told him of her riding lessons with Señor Roberto, who used to be with Sims' Circus.

"So that's where Roberto is," Dan Webster exclaimed. "I wondered where he'd gone. I'd like to run out to see him tomorrow morning. What's the address of his riding academy?"

Nancy gave him directions, then left Dan to find Ned. When Nancy showed Ned the tickets, he shook his head in amazement. "I might have known you would accomplish the impossible."

The seats were in the front row of a box directly along the tanbark. To her surprise, Nancy noticed that the other seats in the box were empty. With the house sold out, why had no one claimed them?

Nancy watched eagerly for the clowns to appear. Every one of them came out except Pietro.

"Maybe Kroon is responsible," Nancy thought.

A few moments later Kroon stepped to the center of the ring and announced that the next performance would be a horse act.

"This is the world's smartest horse!" the ringmaster proclaimed. "He thinks like a human being."

All the lights went out except the spotlight on the ring. A beautiful pure-white horse trotted in from the wings.

Nancy was vaguely aware that a man had slid into the seat directly behind her. But she was too intrigued by the beautiful horse to pay attention to the latecomer. Suddenly she felt something tighten against her throat. She was being choked!

Nancy's hand flew to her throat. To her horror she felt a cord around her neck. It was being drawn tighter and tighter.

Objects swam before Nancy's eyes. With a gasp she reached for Ned's arm, then fainted. Ned turned. Horrified, he quickly unwound the cord.

"Nancy!" he cried. "Are you all right?"

Quickly Ned massaged her neck and arms. In a few minutes Nancy sat up and looked around questioningly.

"Nancy, are you all right?" Ned repeated anxiously.

"Y-yes. What happened to me?"

He told her, pointing to a souvenir whip on the floor. Then he added, "It must have been the work of a maniac!"

Suddenly remembering the man who had sat down behind her, Nancy turned around. The seat was vacant. Nancy questioned a woman in the box directly behind theirs, but although she admitted having seen a man come in and leave, she could not give a description of him. Ned hurried off to report the incident to the police.

Nancy picked up the short whip. It was the type sold as souvenirs at the circus. Calling to a nearby vendor, Nancy asked if he had sold a whip to a man who was sitting behind her.

"Naw," the vendor replied disgustedly. "I ain't sold one of them all evening!"

When Ned returned, Nancy whispered to him, "I think the choker was somebody connected with the circus."

Ned agreed and added the thought that the box might be reserved for circus personnel.

Shortly after that the Cinderella act began. The handsome prince whom she had promised to marry while at the ball swung gracefully to her

Nancy was being choked!

platform. In his hand was a glass slipper. When he found that it fitted Lolita's foot, he embraced her. Then came a fascinating trapeze act, with the two swinging back and forth, first alone, then together.

The sides of the gleaming coach and the two white steeds and Cinderella's spangled dress were drawn up by pulleys. Lolita put on the beautiful white ball gown as the pumpkin and mice were covered by the stately carriage and horses. Then she and her prince stepped inside and were brought down to the ground. They emerged from the coach and took bow after bow amid thunderous applause. Lolita looked in Nancy's direction and blew her a kiss.

"That was superb," Ned remarked when the couple had hurried out of the ring. "Anything else would be tame. How about leaving, Nancy?"

Nancy agreed. "I want to find out about this box," she said. "That man must have had a ticket to it."

The ticket booth was closed, but Nancy saw an attendant and asked him who owned Box AA.

When he told her that it was kept by the circus management for special people, Nancy said to Ned, "Now I'm convinced that my attacker was someone who works here."

"But why would anyone try to choke you?" Ned asked.

Neither could answer this question. Nancy

went up to one of the clowns and inquired about Pietro. When she heard that he had been ill, Nancy asked, "Would you mind giving him a note?"

"Glad to," the clown replied.

Taking paper and pencil from her bag, Nancy quickly scribbled a message. In it she asked Pietro if he could bring Lolita to her house between shows the next day. She wished to talk about finding Lolita's mother.

It was late when Nancy arrived home and said good night to Ned. As soon as she reached her room, the young detective's mind went back to her harrowing experience with the whip.

As she pulled her dress over her head, a wild thought struck Nancy. Had Kroon found out she was interested in helping Lolita and therefore was afraid some sinister affairs of his own might be uncovered? If so, he might want to put a stop to her work.

As Nancy looked down at the floor, she saw a small folded piece of paper. It must have dropped from her dress, she thought. Puzzled, she picked it up and opened the sheet. Nancy stared at the crudely printed message:

STAY AWAY FROM THE CIRCUS AND EVERYONE IN IT!

CHAPTER VI

Stunt Riding

DUMFOUNDED, Nancy reread the warning. The would-be strangler must have slipped the note into the pocket of her dress!

"Of course I won't pay any attention," she resolved, "but I'd better be on my guard."

The next morning Nancy went to the academy for her lesson with Señor Roberto. When he left the ring to answer the telephone, she continued to practice somersaulting from her horse.

As Nancy halted Belgian Star, she saw Dan Webster, the horse trainer from Sims' Circus, standing in the doorway. He nodded and called out, "Very fine riding, Nancy."

Nancy somersaulted from Belgian Star's back and walked over to the man.

"Say," he remarked admiringly, "if anything should go wrong with our bareback act, I'll call on you as a substitute. How about it?"

Nancy was sure he was teasing her and she laughed gaily. The horse trainer did not smile.

"I'm serious," he insisted. "You're as good as many of the circus riders."

At that moment Señor Roberto returned from his office. Seeing his old friend Dan Webster, he threw his arms about the man.

"It is good to see you, *amigo mio*. How are things at Sims'?"

Dan Webster's face clouded. "Not so good. Since you left, things have been getting worse," he replied.

"You mean because of Kroon?" Roberto asked.

Webster nodded. Then he smiled. "I've been talking to your young pupil here. She is an excellent horsewoman."

When Roberto agreed, the horse trainer repeated his suggestion that Nancy substitute as a bareback rider in the circus.

Roberto looked startled, then laughed. "You'll never get Nancy Drew to be a circus rider. She's a detective."

It was Dan Webster's turn to look surprised. "You have actually solved cases?" he asked.

Nancy smiled. "I love mysteries," she said, "and I like nothing better than to work on one."

The horse trainer looked at her intently. "In that case," he said, "perhaps you can solve the mystery of Sims' Circus."

Nancy looked at Señor Roberto and said half-reproachfully, "You never told me there was a mystery at Sims' Circus."

"I did not know it myself," Roberto replied. The riding master explained he had left the circus because he could not get along with Reinhold Kroon. His decision did not involve any mystery.

"What has happened since I left the circus, Dan?" he asked.

Webster explained that Kroon's personality was an odd mixture. He could be delightful and charming one moment and hard and cruel the next. The circus people both admired and hated him.

"Why is that?" Nancy asked.

"Well, it's hard to say. Kroon almost seems to hypnotize folks. He orders them to do impossible things and they do them. Take Lolita, for instance. Actually she's scared of the high wire, but when her father insists, she goes ahead with her performance."

Dan Webster went on to say that Sims, who owned the circus, was like putty in Kroon's hands. He took orders from the ringmaster!

"I can't figure it out," the horse trainer said. "It's almost as if Kroon has some evil hold over Sims and Lolita, and even Mrs. Kroon."

Nancy asked if Mrs. Kroon were one of the performers.

"She used to be a bareback rider," Dan Webster replied. "But she got too heavy. Now she just helps her husband and her daughter. Once in a while she speaks as if she is about to get something off her mind—and you should see the look Kroon gives her! Then she shuts up like a clam!"

Nancy brought the conversation around to Lolita and Pietro. Webster said he thought they were in love, but that Kroon never let his adopted daughter out of his sight.

"So the two young folks rarely have a chance to be alone," he said. "And between you and me, I'm afraid Kroon and the circus would fold up if Lolita should ever leave."

After a pause, Dan Webster turned to Nancy and asked if she would try another stunt. "A somersault across the horse's back while it's moving," he said. "Want to try it?"

Nancy hesitated. Then she said that perhaps the stunt was not so difficult as it looked. It would depend on correct timing.

"You're absolutely right," he said. "Watch the rhythm of the horse's gait. Hum a tune to Belgian Star's slow canter. Then decide exactly from which point you should start to run. When you're sure of your timing, take a few steps toward the horse, place your head and shoulders on the mare's back, and over you go."

Roberto insisted that Nancy put on a padded jacket and hat before attempting the trick. Then, with precision timing, Nancy did the somersault perfectly.

"Splendid!" Webster cried jubilantly. From his pocket he pulled out a ticket to the afternoon performance of the circus.

"Come to the show and watch the bareback riding very carefully," he said.

Nancy thanked him, said good-by to the two men, and drove home. She found Hannah Gruen busy in the kitchen, preparing lunch.

"Oh, that soufflé looks yummy!" Nancy exclaimed as the housekeeper took a puffy, delicious-smelling dish from the oven.

"We'll sit right down and eat," Hannah stated. "Nothing should interrupt a soufflé."

As if to belie her words, the front doorbell rang. As Nancy hastened to answer it, Hannah called, "Now don't let anyone ruin our lunch!"

Nancy laughed sympathetically. Meals in the Drew household were forever being interrupted by Mr. Drew's law cases and Nancy's mysteries.

Opening the door, Nancy saw a young couple she did not recognize. The girl was attractively dressed and wore a scarf that nearly hid her face.

"Please let us in quickly!" she said, stepping into the hall.

Suddenly Nancy recognized her caller. "Lolita!" she exclaimed. "I'm sorry I didn't know you at first. You look so different in street clothes."

"I rarely wear them," the aerialist replied. Then, seeing that Nancy did not recognize her escort, she said with a laugh, "I'd like to present my fiancé, Pietro."

Nancy's eyes opened wide. The clown was a very handsome man with features quite unlike the garishly painted ones Nancy remembered from his trick act on the ladder.

"I certainly didn't know you, Pietro," she said, smiling. "I think it's wonderful you two are engaged."

Lolita confided that they had just decided to be married. "There are two obstacles in my way, though," she said. "One is my foster father. He will never consent to my marriage."

"What is the other problem?" Nancy asked.

The young aerialist said that she wanted to learn more about her own father and mother before she married. And if her parents, or one of them, were alive, she wanted them to attend her wedding.

"The Kroons never legally adopted me," Lolita continued. "They have always told me I belonged to them. Recently I found out I don't."

"Did the Kroons tell you that?" Nancy asked.

"Oh, goodness, no," Lolita replied. "Pietro, you fill Nancy in on the details."

The young man explained that his father, a retired clown, had been in Sims' Circus with The Flying Flanders. He had told Pietro that Lolita's parents had had an accident in their trapeze act and had been taken to the hospital. There, according to Kroon, they had died. Mr. and Mrs. Kroon had taken Lolita, although they had never really adopted her.

"Just this morning I had a letter from my father, who lives in England. He said that while attending a circus in the town of Tewkesbury, he had seen a woman in the audience he was sure was Lolita's mother," Pietro continued.

"Isn't that exciting?" Lolita cried.

"It certainly is," Nancy said. "Go on, Pietro."

The clown said his father had hurried to speak to the woman but that she had disappeared before he could reach her.

"As soon as I read this, I told Mr. Kroon," Pietro said. "But instead of being glad that Lolita's mother might be alive, he flew into a rage and forbade me to speak to Lolita!"

His fiancée added, "The only reason we could get away today was because Mr. Sims has returned, and Mr. Kroon is having a conference with him. We have to hurry back. But you will help me to find my mother, won't you?"

"I certainly will," Nancy assured her. "My father is a lawyer. He might be able to learn something through friends in England."

Lolita said that would be wonderful. Before the couple left, Nancy said she expected to attend the afternoon performance and asked Lolita if it would be possible to talk to Mrs. Kroon.

"Do try, Nancy," Lolita replied. "She'll probably be in my trailer."

As soon as Hannah Gruen heard the front door close, she burst into a mild tirade about strangers who arrive at mealtime. Nancy laughed and sat down to eat the soufflé, which had not caved in and was delicious.

The young sleuth arrived early at the circus and went at once to see Mrs. Kroon. She purposely wore her new charm bracelet. Although Mrs. Kroon eyed it, she made no comment.

After a few general remarks, Nancy asked the woman, "Did your daughter inherit her aerial talent from you?"

Instantly Mrs. Kroon's expression changed from pleasantness to anger. Instead of replying, she cried, "How did you get in here? Our private lives are our own business! I do not intend to answer personal questions!"

"I'm sorry," Nancy said. "Please forgive me." She backed out of the trailer.

Several circus performers were standing around and had evidently overheard the conversation. One of the women spoke in a low voice. "Don't mind Mrs. Kroon. Lolita's her adopted daughter and she's awful touchy on the subject."

"I see," said Nancy. "Are Lolita's real parents living?"

The woman hesitated, then said, "There's a story going around here that Lolita's mother is alive and the Kroons don't want anyone to know. Personally, we think there's something very strange about the whole thing."

Nancy thanked her informer and hurried to her seat in the big top. As she waited for the show to begin, Nancy mulled over various angles of the mystery. Had Lola Flanders pawned the bracelet? Was she the person who needed help? Were the Kroons the cause of her trouble?

Nancy was brought out of her reverie by the band striking up. The performance began. Leaning forward in her seat, she paid particular attention to the bareback-riding act. The riders were experts in timing themselves to the movements of the horses. One attractive girl rider was more proficient than the others and did a great deal of solo work.

This young rider had just completed a midair double somersault and landed on the horse's back amid tumultuous applause when an object hurtled through the air hit the horse on the nose. The mare reared, throwing the young girl.

At once there was confusion among the other horses and their riders. In the midst of the chaos, Nancy spotted the object that had struck the horse.

A whip, exactly like the one her assailant had used, was lying on the tanbark!

CHAPTER VII

Meeting a Challenge

THE injured bareback rider tried to stand, but it was evident at once that her ankle was either badly sprained or broken. Her face was creased with pain. Two riders stepped forward. She put an arm around the shoulders of each man, and they helped her from the ring. Meanwhile, her horse had run to the exit.

The remaining performers carried on, doing their best, but it was apparent that the mishap had made them nervous. At a signal from the band, inspired by Kroon, the act came to an abrupt end.

The whip that had caused the accident had been kicked out of the way and seemed to have been forgotten by everyone but Nancy.

"I thought the person who tried to strangle me had a grudge against me personally," she mused.

"But what could his motive have been for injuring the circus rider?"

Recalling her first suspicions of the stableman at Roberto's riding academy, Nancy wondered if it was possible that Hitch had perpetrated all three bits of mischief.

"Hitch did warn me not to do any circus riding," Nancy reminded herself. "Maybe he doesn't want other girls to, either."

As the next act was announced, Nancy saw Chief of Police McGinnis of the River Heights force walk into the box she had occupied the evening before. He was wearing civilian clothes. Getting up, she hurried over and sat beside him.

"Hello, Nancy," he said genially. "What's the mystery this time? Whenever you seek me out, I know something's in the wind!"

Nancy smiled and confessed that she did have a problem. She asked if he had reached the circus in time to see what had happened to the young bareback rider.

"No," the chief replied, "but the guard outside told me about the accident. Too bad. I was hoping the circus would get through the three days here without any trouble. But I suppose we have to expect such things."

"It's my idea," Nancy said thoughtfully, "that it was a deliberate attempt to injure the girl and her horse."

"What makes you think so?" the officer asked.

Nancy told him what had happened to her the evening before with the very same kind of whip.

The chief whistled. "Why didn't you tell me this before now?" he demanded.

Nancy explained that Ned had spoken to the circus policeman. "And we did search for the man," she added.

Chief McGinnis, who admired Nancy's ability as a detective, remarked, "If you couldn't find the man, it was probably because he skipped out."

"I also had a threatening note from the strangler," Nancy went on. "I was going to bring it to you, but so many things have happened since then that I've had no chance. I did look it over carefully, Chief, and couldn't find a clue to the writer."

"Well," he said, smiling, "we'll call your findings the preliminary investigation. Bring the note to headquarters. I'd like to give it a microscopic test."

Nancy promised to do so, then told Chief McGinnis her suspicions about Hitch. After she mentioned the stableman's warning about stunt riding and the incident of the stone throwing, the officer advised Nancy to be wary.

"I certainly think you have good reason to suspect that fellow Hitch," he said. "I'll put a detail on him right away."

Nancy returned to her seat and concentrated on Lolita's act. The performance went off exceedingly well. When it ended and while Nancy was applauding with the enthusiastic crowd, an usher came up to her with a note.

As she started to open it, Nancy's breath came a little faster. Was this another warning? Had her unknown enemy seen her talking to the Chief of Police?

A moment later the girl's fears were allayed. The note was from Dan Webster, asking her to meet him in his office at once.

Nancy rose and hurried from the tent. A hundred thoughts flashed through her mind before she reached the office. What could he want of her? As she walked in, Dan Webster smiled and offered her a chair. Then, looking directly at her, he said, "I won't beat around the bush, Nancy. I want you to take the place of that injured bareback rider."

Nancy was so amazed she opened her mouth and closed it again without speaking. Then she managed to exclaim, "You want me to take that girl's place!"

"I told you this morning that you ride well enough to be in the circus."

"But I can't perform like that girl!" Nancy objected. "She's excellent. By the way, how is she?"

Webster revealed that the young rider's ankle had been sprained in the fall. The doctor had advised her to keep off her ankle for at least a month.

"Oh, what a shame!" Nancy cried, then added, "Thank you very much for your compliment, but, really, I'll have to refuse. Even if I could do the riding, I know Mr. Kroon would never approve of my joining Sims' Circus."

The horse trainer said he did not think the ringmaster would disapprove. Furthermore, Kroon had given an ultimatum that the bareback act was to be filled in before the evening show or the whole troupe would be dismissed.

"The actors might change their routine, but unfortunately the horses can't," Webster told her. "It takes a long time to train them and there's no changing 'em."

Nancy felt sorry for the group that depended on the act for their livelihood. If she could ride for one or two performances, until they found a replacement, it might help.

Dan Webster took her silence as a sign of refusal. Leaning toward her, he said in a whisper, "You know, this might be your golden opportunity to solve the mystery of the circus. If you lived with us for a week or so, you could watch the Kroons at close range."

This plea did the trick. Laughing, Nancy said she would join the circus, provided her father approved.

"He's on a trip, but I'll try to locate him," she promised. "I'm not sure where he is staying at present."

"If you don't," Webster said, "I'll turn this old earth upside down to find him. Where do we start?"

He pushed the telephone toward Nancy and insisted that she begin calling. First she tried Mr. Drew's office, only to learn that they had not heard from him that day and did not know where he was.

As she put the phone down, Lolita and Pietro walked into the office. Nancy was surprised to see them together, and Lolita must have guessed her thoughts.

"We're becoming very bold about being seen with each other." The circus star laughed happily.

Pietro frowned. "But look for an explosion if Mr. Kroon sees us!"

"Let's not worry," the aerialist said, adding that all her friends were acting as lookouts and would notify them at once if Lolita's foster father were close by.

"Say," Dan Webster spoke up, "you two will have to help me out. Nancy Drew must take Rosa's place. I have persuaded her, but she tells me she won't join the circus unless her father gives his permission, and we can't locate Mr. Drew. What am I going to do?"

Lolita walked over to Nancy and put an arm around the girl. "I think it would be nice for you to have your father's permission," she said, "but, after all, he doesn't object to your circus riding at Señor Roberto's, does he?"

"No."

"Then what's the difference whether you're riding in our ring or the one at the riding academy?" Lolita asked persuasively.

"I don't suppose there is any," Nancy agreed, "but I'd still like to get in touch with him. I have an idea. Two friends of mine who often work with me will be glad to try to locate him, I'm sure. In the meantime, I'll practice some stunt riding. After all, I haven't ridden with the other members of the bareback troupe. The whole thing might be a flop with me in it."

"Oh, no, it couldn't be!" Lolita cried excitedly.

Dan Webster said that the members of the equestrian group were meeting in twenty minutes to decide what to do about the act. If Nancy would come to the main tent at that time, he would introduce her and let them see her work.

"I'll find you some riding clothes, Nancy," Lolita offered. "Come on!"

Before leaving the office, Nancy telephoned Bess and George, who, she knew, were at Roberto's academy. They were overwhelmed to hear that their friend planned to ride in the circus. Bess begged Nancy to reconsider, but finally she promised to help locate Mr. Drew.

"Thanks a million," said Nancy. "And hurry."

"Express service." George laughed as she put down the telephone.

Nancy and Lolita left Webster's office with Pietro. They had gone only a few steps when one of the midgets rushed up to Lolita.

"Your father's coming!" he warned.

With that, Pietro dodged behind a truck. The two girls went on. A moment later they were confronted by Kroon.

"Who is this, Lolita?" he asked sternly. Giving Nancy a piercing look, he said, "Aren't you the girl who let that kid sneak a ride in Cinderella's carriage during the parade?"

The ringmaster did not wait for Nancy to answer. His eyes flashing, he ordered her to leave the circus grounds at once. Then, turning to Lolita, he snapped, "Get to your trailer and don't come out until suppertime!"

Over Kroon's shoulder, Nancy spotted Pietro. He was beckoning her. His signal seemed to indicate that she was to pretend to leave and that he would follow and meet her later. After bidding Lolita good-by, Nancy started off. Kroon stood there until he was sure his daughter had obeyed his command; then he stalked away.

A short distance farther, Pietro caught up with Nancy. He offered to guide her to the trailer where extra costumes were kept, including riding habits.

Nancy shook her head. "It wouldn't be safe

now, Pietro. I suspect that Mr. Kroon knows who I am. I think he mentioned Teddy as an excuse for ordering me to leave. He doesn't want me around here and will do anything to keep me away."

Pietro looked crestfallen. After a moment of silence, he said, "Even so, Nancy, you must stay and see what you can do for Lolita and me. Listen! I'm going to tell you something that I don't even dare tell my fiancée. She would be worried sick.

"I was walking past Mr. and Mrs. Kroon's trailer a little while ago. I believe they thought nobody was around. Mrs. Kroon was crying and saying to her husband, 'The money won't do us any good if people find out where it came from.' "

Nancy was startled. "Have you any idea what Mrs. Kroon meant?" she asked the clown, but he shook his head.

Nancy's mind jumped to one possibility. The Kroons may have secretly gained possession of money that did not rightfully belong to them!

CHAPTER VIII

A Quick Switch

THERE was no question now in Nancy Drew's mind that if she rode in the circus act she would be in danger—and not only from the angle of riding. Intuition told her there would be other hazards as well!

"I'll need eyes in the back of my head," the girl thought.

"Please don't let us down," Pietro pleaded. "You see what a dreadful position Lolita is in. Even if we ran away and got married, I don't think it would solve our problem. Kroon might continue to make life miserable for us."

"I agree," Nancy answered. "I'll do everything I can for you and Lolita. But if my father disapproves of my living at the circus, I'll have to work on the outside."

The clown thanked Nancy and then took her to

Mrs. Kelly, the wardrobe mistress. Nancy was quickly outfitted in dark-blue jodhpurs and a white blouse. But instead of boots she was given soft heelless slippers. Since she had never used this kind of footwear in stunt riding, Nancy asked Mrs. Kelly about them.

"That's what all our bareback riders use," Mrs. Kelly replied. "You'll probably find them easier to manage than stiff boots."

After thanking the woman, Nancy hurried to the Big Top where Dan Webster awaited her. He introduced the equestrian group and their leader, Rancoco.

Dan took the arm of an attractive young woman with lovely blond hair and big blue eyes. "Erika will be your roommate when you join us," he said.

The two girls smiled at each other, then Nancy asked, "What shall I do first?"

Fortunately, the lead horse, whose nose had been bruised, was all right otherwise. She was the same size and build as Belgian Star, so when Nancy swung herself onto the mare's back, she felt almost as if she were riding Roberto's thoroughbred.

"Now, don't be nervous," Webster encouraged. "Just do those stunts I saw you performing at Roberto's and you'll be all right."

Despite his reassurance, Nancy was tense. At

first she performed the stunts stiffly, but when Erika reminded her to relax, the riding went better.

"Well, what do you think?" Dan asked Rancoco when Nancy had finished.

"For a girl not reared in the circus, she surely is remarkable," the leader replied. "Even if she can't join us permanently, I'll be glad to take her on until we can get a substitute for Rosa."

He asked Nancy if she had ever stood on a cantering horse with another person.

"No. I haven't."

Rancoco suggested she try it with him after watching another couple do the stunt. Nancy consented, and when they were ready, he said, "You go first."

Nancy timed the rhythm of the horse, ran several steps across the ring, and hopped onto her mare's back. A moment later Rancoco joined her. But as he touched her, Nancy lost her balance and off they both fell!

"Not hurt, are you?" he asked, helping her up. Nancy shook her head gamely. "Better luck next time," he said with an encouraging smile.

Nancy had several more spills, but finally she was able to steady herself when Rancoco hopped up behind her.

"Fine, fine!" he praised her. "If you do your part as well tonight, everything will be okay."

At that moment Pietro raced into the tent. "Kroon's coming!" he cried in great agitation. "He suspects something funny is going on. He's in a rage and says he'll fire all of you for double-crossing him!"

"Pietro, he must have found out about me," Nancy said in dismay.

The clown's face was dark with anger. "I'm afraid so. There's a spy in this circus, and I'm going to find out who he is!"

Before Pietro could say any more, Bess Marvin rushed into the tent. Seeing her in riding clothes gave Nancy an idea. Without waiting to hear why Bess had come, Nancy said to her, "Kroon's coming in here any minute. He must have heard I'm trying out for a part in this act. He mustn't see me. You'll have to take my place!"

Poor Bess had no time to make a choice. As Nancy dived behind some seats, the ringmaster walked in. He strode over to Bess.

"So you're the girl who's trying out, eh?"

"Why—uh, yes," Bess replied.

"I thought it was somebody else," he said. Then he added, "You don't look like much of a rider, but get up on the mare and let's see what you can do."

Obediently Bess mounted. She felt sick with fear and only her loyalty to Nancy gave her the courage to carry on.

Bess rode well and Kroon seemed to be impressed. "Now let's see what stunts you can do," he called.

Bess's heart thumped wildly. What could she do? "I—I can't work in these clothes," she stammered. "Could you come back in an hour, Mr. Kroon?"

"An hour!" the ringmaster yelled. "An hour to change your clothes? I'll give you exactly half—well, forty-five minutes."

"Thank you," said Bess, sliding from the horse.

Kroon looked at Rancoco. "I want every one of you back here in exactly forty-five minutes. I'll be watching the act. If I don't like it, out you go. This time I won't change my mind!"

As he stalked off, there was silence. The equestrians were too worried to talk, and Nancy realized how much depended on her. She emerged from behind the seats.

Bess begged her not to take part in the bareback act. "You're just going to get yourself in trouble," she insisted. "It isn't worth the risk."

"I can't let these people down now," Nancy replied. "But thanks a million for helping me. Will you give this to Hannah?" she asked, taking off the charm bracelet.

"Sure," Bess replied.

"By the way, Bess, did you find Dad?"

"Yes and no." Bess reported that George had contacted Nancy's Aunt Eloise Drew in New York

City. Miss Drew was expecting her brother and would have him telephone George's home as soon as he arrived.

"Thanks, Bess," said Nancy. "Now how am I going to fool Kroon into thinking I'm you!"

Erika, who overheard the remark, smiled. "It won't be any trouble," she said. "Our makeup artist can fix that. With a blond wig and some stage makeup, you'll fool him all right!"

"Let's start," Nancy urged.

The three girls went off together, and within half an hour Nancy's appearance was considerably changed. As the girls left the makeup tent, they almost bumped into George Fayne. She stared at Nancy as if she had seen a ghost.

"What's been going on?" she exclaimed.

Quickly George was brought up to date, then Nancy asked, "Did Dad call?"

George grinned. She said that Mr. Drew had telephoned and would be happy to let Nancy pinch-hit in the circus act.

"What's more," George added, "your aunt is flying in with him to see tonight's performance."

"How wonderful!" Nancy cried. Then it suddenly occurred to her that she had told Hannah she would be home at six o'clock and it was now six thirty. Nancy decided to call her at once.

"I'll invite her to the evening performance," Nancy thought, her eyes dancing. "But I'll keep my part in it a surprise."

After Nancy explained to the housekeeper that she was still at the circus, Hannah Gruen told her that Chief McGinnis had called.

"He says to tell you that fellow Hitch has disappeared. You're to watch your step!"

The news disturbed Nancy. She felt sure that the stableman had run away because he was guilty of the three suspicious incidents.

"Did the chief tell you anything else?" Nancy asked the housekeeper.

"Yes. One of his men found some souvenir whips hidden in Hitch's quarters. And he told me that Hitch had tried to strangle you. You must be careful, Nancy. That fellow's clothes are still at the stable, which means he probably hasn't gone far."

Nancy was worried. It occurred to her that Hitch might be lurking around the circus grounds, planning more deviltry. If he were, nobody would be safe.

Aloud Nancy said, "Don't think any more about it. I'm going to stay for the evening circus performance and I'd like you to come. Dad will be here with someone else you like."

Hannah promised to attend, and Nancy said she would leave a ticket for her at the entrance booth. After bidding Hannah good-by, Nancy went to find Dan Webster. He was pleased to hear that she had her father's approval and promised to have Box AA set aside for her that evening.

When Nancy told him about Hitch and her suspicions that he might be hiding on the circus grounds, Dan's face became livid with anger. "Why that shriveled-up good-for-nothing!" he shouted. "I never did have any use for him. I'll find him! He won't get away with another of his tricks!"

Telling Nancy to go ahead to the big tent, the horse trainer hurried off to start a search. When Nancy arrived at the riding ring, she was delighted to hear that Rancoco had persuaded the ringmaster to view the act from one of the boxes.

"That way he won't be able to tell you aren't the same girl he saw before." Rancoco grinned.

Everything went smoothly and Kroon seemed satisfied with the act. After he had left the tent, Bess came out of hiding. Nancy told her there would be seats for her and George in Box AA. The girls said good-by to Nancy and left for their homes.

Nancy joined Lolita at the cafeteria for supper. Suddenly remembering the conversation between Mr. and Mrs. Kroon that Pietro had overheard, Nancy asked Lolita, "Did your own parents leave any money in trust for you?"

"Oh no," Lolita replied. "In fact Mr. Kroon once told me I was penniless and completely dependent on him."

As she finished speaking, a gong sounded in the cafeteria tent. Lolita explained that it was a signal to the circus people to get ready for the evening performance.

"I must hurry and try on my costume," Nancy said. "See you later."

She walked toward the trailer where earlier she had made a date with Mrs. Kelly, the wardrobe mistress.

"I'm all ready for you," the woman said pleasantly. "This is poor Rosa's costume. Suppose you try it on and we'll see how it fits."

Nancy removed her riding habit and stepped into the white satin ballerina-skirted costume. It was perfect!

A few minutes later Nancy was completely outfitted. Carrying the costume and accessories over her arm, she walked to the supply tent to obtain special makeup.

Placing the costume on a chair near the open doorway, Nancy walked to the rear to find someone to advise her of what she needed. No one was there.

"I'll borrow some makeup from Erika," she decided and turned back to the entrance. As she did she saw the missing stableman! Hitch had Nancy's costume in his hands.

"Put that down!" Nancy cried.

The stableman dashed out the door and disappeared.

CHAPTER IX

A Dangerous Performance

NANCY had to get back her costume! She needed the fancy riding habit for the evening performance!

"Oh, where did Hitch go?" she fumed, looking in every direction.

Seeing a workman taking down one of the small tents, Nancy hastened to him and asked if he had seen a man running from the supply tent.

"No, miss," he replied. "You looking for someone?"

Quickly Nancy told him that she was trying to find a man named Hitch.

"Oh, I know him. He used to be with this circus."

"He took my costume and I must have it," Nancy explained. "Please help me find Hitch and hold him for the police."

"I'll do my best, miss," the workman promised, hurrying away to begin his search.

Nancy decided to speak to Dan Webster and went to his office. The horse trainer was thunderstruck when she told him of the groom's latest bit of deviltry.

"I thought we searched every part of these grounds for Hitch," he said, "and the guards at all entrances were warned not to let him in or out."

Dan Webster picked up his telephone. He called the ticket office and everyone stationed outside the grounds. The last guard to whom he talked said, "Hey, wait a minute! I see something."

A moment later the man reported that he had the missing costume. "It was in a box under one of the booths. I noticed a man put a package there, but didn't know he was Hitch. I'm sure he hasn't left the grounds."

"Then he must be hiding here!" Nancy thought fearfully.

Dan asked the guard to bring the costume to his office at once. While they were waiting for it, he warned Nancy to be watchful every minute until the groom was caught.

When the costume arrived, Nancy found to her relief that it was unharmed. Hitch had evidently grabbed a large box from the supply tent and put the costume and accessories in it so he would not be seen with them.

"Thanks so much," Nancy said to Dan, and she ran off to dress for the performance.

"My goodness, where have you been?" Erika asked when Nancy entered their tent. "It's only fifteen minutes to parade time!"

Nancy told her roommate what had happened. Erika was aghast. "I hope that awful man has left the circus grounds," she said, helping Nancy into her costume. Then the two girls raced to the makeup tent.

The girls had received their last fluffs of face powder when the warning gong sounded. They hurried off and swung onto the backs of their mounts. The band struck up, and a moment later the parade started.

Nancy had never been more excited and nervous in her life. It was thrilling to ride with the circus people, but a fear lurked in her mind that Hitch might be hiding nearby, ready to harm her or one of the other riders.

As Nancy came opposite the box where her father and Aunt Eloise were seated, she noticed to her delight that Hannah, Bess, George, and Ned were there also. They waved to her, but she did not dare acknowledge the greeting. Kroon or one of his spies might be watching.

Finally the parade was over and Ringmaster

Kroon entered the ring to announce the equestrian act.

"Ladies and gentlemen," he began, "you are about to witness some of the world's finest bareback riding. The Vascon family will perform the most daring stunts you have ever witnessed."

Overhearing the announcement in the wings, Nancy smiled. Not only was she not a Vascon or related to any of the other performers, but not one of them was related to any other!

The horses trotted in and took their places in the ring. The performance started, the mares cantering about rhythmically to the music. Singly, and together, the riders did their stunts.

In Box AA, Mr. Drew and his friends kept their eyes riveted on Nancy. "She's wonderful!" Bess exclaimed.

Nancy outdid herself. She made no mistakes, and her performance was excellent. When Rancoco jumped up behind her on the mare and they cantered around the ring, he whispered enthusiastically, "Superb, Nancy. Superb!"

Pleased, Nancy smiled. The show went on without interruption. But just as one of the men riders began his solo, there was a wild scream in the audience.

Turning, the equestrians saw a hard-thrown baseball whizzing from one of the exits directly at them!

Like lightning, each performer pulled his horse to the tanbark and lay down himself. The speeding ball flew over their heads and landed beyond the ring.

The audience was divided in its reaction. Some were stunned. But many people thought it was part of the act and clapped loudly. Their attitude steadied the nerves of the riders and the performance went on.

Later, when Nancy and Erika reached their dressing room, Nancy announced that she was changing to street clothes.

"Where are you going?" her roommate asked.

"I'm not sure," Nancy replied, "but I'm going to try to find Hitch."

"Oh Nancy, do be careful. You must be back in time for the final pageant!"

"How much time will there be before that?" Nancy asked.

Erika glanced at the clock. "Two and a half hours."

"I'll be back in time," said Nancy, and she left the dressing room.

She asked Dan Webster if the ball thrower had been captured and was told that he had escaped. "It was probably Hitch," the horse trainer said ruefully. "He's still at large."

Nancy went to Box AA. Mr. Drew and the others whispered that she had been a sensation.

Nancy smiled and slid into a seat beside Ned. She asked him if he would accompany her on a little sleuthing expedition.

"Of course," he replied. "Where?"

"Roberto's stables," she said, and then she told him about the missing stableman. "Hitch's clothes are still at the place. He may be hiding there."

Nancy whispered to her father that she and Ned would be gone for a short time and told him not to worry about them. Then she and Ned got into his car and drove to the riding academy.

"This place is as dark as a tomb," Ned remarked, "and just about as cheerful."

He parked a short distance from the stable and the couple walked quietly toward it. They were halfway to the rear entrance when Nancy grabbed Ned's arm.

"Listen!"

The sound of hoofbeats and frightened whinnies reached their ears.

"Someone is trying to steal Belgian Star!" Nancy exclaimed.

Nancy and Ned raced toward the riding academy. In the dim light they caught a glimpse of horse and rider disappearing down the road.

"I'm sure that's Belgian Star!" Nancy cried. "We must catch her."

"Come on!" Ned cried. "We'll chase them in the car."

They hurried back and hopped into the car. The two rode in silence until they heard the rhythmic beat of a horse's hoofs on the road ahead of them.

The rider must have guessed that he was being pursued. Reaching an open field, he turned sharply and raced directly across it.

Ned did the same. The ground was soft and rutted, but he drove on doggedly until they came to a brook with a thick woods on the other side.

Nancy jumped out of the car and called at the top of her voice, "Star! Whoa! Come back!"

The mare must have heard Nancy. The hoof-beats and crashing of underbrush stopped. Nancy and Ned heard a frantic "Giddap! Giddap!" But there was still no sound from the horse.

Quickly Nancy reached into the car and pulled a flashlight from the glove compartment. She turned it on and waved it back and forth high in the air. "Star!" she called, "come back!"

Suddenly there was a sound of hoofbeats. A moment later the car's headlights picked up the oncoming horse. It was Belgian Star with Hitch, the groom, astride her!

The mare stopped at the edge of the brook. In desperation, Hitch jumped from Belgian Star and ran off into the woods.

"I'll get that guy!" Ned yelled. He waded into the stream. When he reached the other side, he plunged into the woods after his quarry.

Belgian Star crossed the stream and came to stand quietly at Nancy's side. Nancy was stroking the horse when she heard a yell. Quickly she mounted the mare, rode across the stream and into the woods.

Playing the flashlight around she caught sight of Ned. He was kneeling beside Hitch, who seemed to be unconscious.

"Just as I reached him, he stumbled and fell," Ned explained. "He hit his head on a stone and blacked out."

Nancy and Ned managed to swing the unconscious man across Belgian Star's back and made their way to the car. There they held a consultation. Ned would ride the horse with Hitch while Nancy drove the car back to the riding academy.

Hitch did not regain consciousness until after Ned had carried him inside the building and laid him on the floor. Together, Nancy and Ned securely tied their prisoner with pieces of harness.

Screaming like a madman, Hitch cried out that he had done nothing and they had no right to tie him.

"Hitch," said Ned, "you have plenty to account for. You'd better start talking."

The groom insisted he had nothing to say.

"If you don't want to tell us, you can give your story to the police," Nancy said, heading for a pay telephone that hung on the wall.

"Star, come back!" Nancy called.

Ned followed her. "I'll call Chief McGinnis," he offered. "You see if you can get anything out of Hitch."

Returning to the prisoner, Nancy asked him why he had tried to strangle her with the whip at the circus.

The man's eyes bulged from his head. "How'd you know I did that?" he asked.

"And why did you throw the stone at me and the ball at the circus rider, except that you don't like people to do trick riding?" she went on.

"I ain't talkin'."

Ned returned to say that Chief McGinnis himself was coming to take charge of Hitch. Nancy and Ned walked over to the door to watch for him.

Presently Ned remarked, "I'm surprised these valuable horses are left unguarded."

"You're right," said Nancy. "Roberto has an apartment upstairs. He must be away."

Suddenly a frightening thought came to Nancy. "Ned," she said, "I'm worried. Would you mind going upstairs to be sure Roberto is not there?"

Ned looked at her, reading her mind. Without replying, he clicked on a second-floor light and dashed up the narrow stairs that led from the stable.

A moment later he cried out, "Nancy, come up here quickly!"

CHAPTER X

The Clue in the Scrapbook

NANCY winced at the sight that met her eyes when she reached the second floor. There lay Señor Roberto, bound and gagged!

He wore no shirt and across his chest, his face, and neck were a series of red, angry welts. He had been whipped!

Ned removed the gag. Nancy sprang forward to help untie the bonds that held the man's arms close to his side. Next, they cut the cords that bound his ankles together.

"I'll get some water," Nancy offered, "and see if I can find the first-aid kit."

"I think Roberto should go to a hospital," Ned told her.

"The police will be here any minute. Perhaps they'll take him," she suggested.

On the first floor of the stable, Nancy found a

first-aid kit. She carried it upstairs and used an antiseptic salve on the riding master's welts. Ned held aromatic spirits of ammonia near the man's nostrils.

But Roberto did not regain consciousness. Nancy and Ned were relieved when Captain McGinnis and two policemen arrived in a police ambulance. Since Hitch was well tied, they turned their attention to Señor Roberto.

"This man is in bad shape," the chief remarked. "Clem," he said, addressing one of his men, "drive Señor Roberto to the hospital at once, and then return here."

The two policemen carried the riding master to their car and drove off.

Chief McGinnis turned to Hitch. He asked Nancy and Ned if the man was responsible for Roberto's condition.

"We haven't had a chance to ask him," said Nancy. "We just found Señor Roberto a few minutes ago."

The chief, with Ned's help, removed the straps from the groom. The officer gazed in silence at the man. Hitch muttered that he knew nothing about what had happened to Señor Roberto. The officer advised the prisoner of his rights.

"If you told the whole story," Chief McGinnis said, glancing at Hitch, "it would go easier on you in court."

Hitch, stiffening at the remark, became sullen. For several minutes he said nothing. Nancy hoped he would break his silence and was relieved when he finally broke down. Hitch suddenly cried out, "I hate Sims' Circus and everybody in it!"

"Why?" the officer asked him.

"Circuses are evil things. Everybody who runs 'em is crazy! Now take Kroon," he said.

As Hitch mentioned the ringmaster's name, Nancy leaned forward to catch every word.

"That ringmaster—he puts up a big front, but he's the biggest thief in the world."

"How do you know?" McGinnis asked him.

Suddenly Hitch became sullen again. He said he could tell plenty about Kroon and everybody else at Sims' Circus, but why should he? What would it get him? They were the people who ought to be going to jail, not he.

The next moment, Hitch gave the most blood-curdling yell Nancy had ever heard. It sent shivers down her spine. Just as the scream ended in a choked gurgle. Hitch dashed for the door. But Ned and Chief McGinnis were on him, and the prisoner did not get far.

"Take it easy, Hitch," the officer advised. "I guess I'll have to put bracelets on you."

The chief pulled handcuffs from his pocket and snapped them on the stableman's wrists. He led the prisoner to a chair and ordered him to sit there quietly until the policemen returned.

Nancy heard a clock begin to strike. She counted the strokes and then cried out, "Ned, the circus! I must get back at once or I'll be late!"

She had only twenty minutes to reach the circus, change her clothes, and appear in the finale.

Before leaving, Nancy said to the chief, "I'd like to come to the jail and talk to Hitch in the morning, if I may."

"Good idea," he told her. "I'll look for you."

The young couple dashed off. As soon as they reached the highway, Ned gave the car full power and it sped along. They had gone only about a mile when a police motorcycle roared up alongside them. Its rider signaled for them to stop.

Nancy's heart sank. She knew the car had been traveling beyond the legal speed limit. A delay would mean that she would miss the circus finale! If Kroon noticed her absence, the whole Vascon troupe might lose their jobs that night!

"Oh, officer," Nancy said quickly, leaning out of the window, "I'm one of the circus performers and I have to get back for the finale at once."

The motorcycle policeman looked at the girl intently for a moment, then said, "If you hadn't told me that, I would have said you were Nancy Drew of River Heights."

Both Nancy and Ned laughed. The girl admitted that she was Nancy Drew and quickly told the officer about her part in the circus and the reason for it.

"What's more," Ned added, "Nancy has just captured that stableman the police were looking for."

The officer asked for details of the capture. Though Nancy begrudged the time it took to tell the story, it turned out to be time well spent. The officer excused Ned for speeding and offered to lead the way directly to the circus.

A few minutes later they reached Sims' Circus. As Nancy hopped out of Ned's car she arranged to meet him at the main gate later. Then she thanked the officer for his help and dashed through the entrance stile.

Erika was nervously waiting for her. She literally peeled Nancy out of her street clothes, helped her put on her riding costume, and pulled on her wig. There was no time to visit the makeup artist, so the girls quickly retouched Nancy's makeup.

By the time they reached the starting point for the pageant, everyone had assembled. As Nancy's group rode around for a final bow, the applause was loud and genuine. Nancy stole a quick look at her father and friends. They were clapping and waving madly.

This was the last performance in River Heights. The next day Sims' Circus would open at a town called Danford. Nancy hoped it would have as warm a reception as it had had in River Heights.

When she and Erika reached their tent, the young detective began to put on her street clothes. Erika asked why she was doing this.

"I'm going home. I'll see you in Danford to-morrow."

Erika looked worried. "It's against the rules for anyone to leave the circus overnight," she said.

"But I'm not a regular member of the troupe," Nancy replied. "I'm sure it won't make any difference if I return home for the night."

Erika advised her to speak to Dan Webster. Nancy went to his office and fortunately found him there.

He instantly agreed with Erika. "Kroon has an insidious way of checking up on folks around here," the horse trainer told Nancy. "It would be much safer if you moved with the circus. We're leaving tonight, you know."

"Tonight?" Nancy said. "You mean we don't sleep here?"

Dan Webster laughed. He said Nancy had a lot to learn about circus life. By the time she returned home, the tents would be down and the performers and workmen in buses and trucks on their way to Danford.

"But I'll need extra clothes," Nancy said. "How am I going to get them?"

Dan advised her to telephone her home at once and have someone bring a suitcase to her within the next fifteen minutes.

Nancy hurried from the office and went directly to the main gate, where she had asked Ned Nickerson to wait for her. He was there, watching in fascination as the big top suddenly swooped to the ground.

"I see this place is packing up," he remarked, as Nancy joined him.

"And I am too," Nancy said, quickly explaining what she had been told to do. "Ned, I'll telephone my house and have Hannah pack a suitcase. She should be home by now. Will you dash over there and bring it back to me? I'll meet you here in fifteen minutes."

"It sounds like a big order—packing any girl's suitcase in that short a time." He laughed. "But I'll be here."

Ned kept his promise and was back with the suitcase in record time. He reluctantly said good-by to Nancy, and added that he would be very willing to drive to Danford if she needed him.

"You're a dear," she said, smiling. "If I need your help, I'll let you know."

Nancy waved good-by and hurried back to

Erika. The rider was wearing a long, attractive dressing gown and slippers. She said she preferred traveling this way since she would have to sleep all night in the bus.

A few moments later a truck came by and picked up the girls' suitcases. Then the Vascon troupe hurried to board the bus that had been assigned to them.

Nancy hardly slept during the trip. The ride was bumpy and the bus stuffy. At Kroon's insistence the circus group stayed together. This meant that they traveled slowly. Every once in a while one of the circus's wild animals would cry out and disturb Nancy. But the regular troupers did not seem to mind the commotion and they slept soundly.

The following morning at Danford, Nancy, left to herself, decided to do some investigating. She went from performer to performer, diplomatically asking about the Kroons, the circus itself, and particularly about Lolita's parents. The young sleuth learned little that she did not already know until she came to the oldest of the clowns, a grizzled man named Leo Sanders.

He was seated in front of his tent, looking through a scrapbook. Nancy squatted on the ground beside him, smiled, and chattily began to question him.

"Before I tell you anything I know," he said,

"suppose you tell me why you want the information."

Quickly Nancy explained why she was trying to help Lolita and that she suspected there might be a secret in connection with the girl's early life.

Sanders began to turn the pages of the scrapbook. Reaching a section near the beginning of the book, he laid it face up on Nancy's lap.

"You may find some of the answers here," he said.

CHAPTER XI

A Unique Admission

In the old clown's scrapbook, now on Nancy's lap, were several pictures of performers and acts of the circus in which Lolita's parents and Sanders had appeared. Poised in flight on a double trapeze were a dainty woman and a handsome man. Under the photograph was the caption:

JOHN AND LOLA FLANDERS

"They were a very talented couple," the old clown remarked wistfully. "Too bad about their accident. For some reason it was hushed up."

There were various other pictures of the famous couple performing their difficult stunts. Nancy could see that Lolita had indeed inherited her great talent from them.

"Yes, it was tragic that they fell," Nancy replied.

"Mr. Sanders, can you tell me anything more about them?"

For answer, the man turned the page of the scrapbook. The two following pages were filled with clippings from European newspapers. None of them was in English, but the old clown helped Nancy translate them. All gave practically the same account. John Flanders had been killed outright. The injuries to his wife had been very serious and she had not been expected to live.

"But none of these clippings," said Nancy, "tell whether or not Mrs. Flanders did recover."

Sanders looked around as if he feared someone might hear what he was about to tell Nancy.

Finally he whispered, "That has been a mystery all these years. One story was that Lola Flanders was taken to England and disappeared."

Nancy's pulse quickened. Probably Pietro's father *had* seen Lola Flanders in Tewkesbury!

Thinking of England reminded Nancy that she had forgotten to ask her father to start his investigation there. She decided that as soon as she finished talking with Leo Sanders, she would telephone the lawyer.

"I've heard," said Nancy, "that John and Lola Flanders were supposed to have had a lot of money. Do you know whether this is true?"

Again Sanders spoke in a low voice. "Yes, the couple made a fortune with their brilliant act.

No one knows what became of the money. Some of the folks around here who don't like Kroon hint that maybe he's handling it and Lolita will never get it."

Nancy wondered about this, but Sanders had nothing further to offer. Nancy then asked the clown whether the Flanders had made all their money in the circus.

"No, not exactly," he replied. "John and Lola were very popular with nobility and other aristocrats in Europe. They were often asked to give special command performances when they were traveling abroad with the circus. They were exceedingly well paid for this."

The clown went on to say that a certain queen was particularly fond of Lola. She had given her beautiful jewelry, including a unique bracelet.

"Please tell me about it," Nancy asked eagerly.

"I only saw it once," Sanders replied, "but I never could forget it. The bracelet was solid gold and had six little horses dangling from it. Five of them represented a different gait. Two were cantering. It was the most artistic piece of jewelry I have ever seen," he concluded. "And now, I understand, you may own this bracelet."

Nancy nodded and added, "I was told that the horse charm Lolita wears on a necklace was given to her by her mother. Do you think it could have come from my bracelet?"

Sanders thought for a moment. He glanced at Nancy as if he were reluctant to say what was on his mind.

Finally he blurted out, "I don't think the one Lolita wears is real. It doesn't glisten as much and isn't so finely made as the ones I saw on her mother's bracelet."

Here was a strange twist, Nancy thought. If the old clown was right, then someone had substituted an imitation horse charm for the lovely one Lolita's mother had given her!

"I'll get my bracelet and compare the horses more closely with Lolita's," Nancy decided. She was positive that hers were the finely wrought originals.

She thanked the clown for his information. Then, before going back to her own tent, she telephoned her father. After giving him the latest news, she asked him to find out what he could in England about Lola Flanders.

Deciding that it was best to keep Sanders' suspicions to herself, Nancy talked with Erika only about the circus itself. Both girls performed expertly that afternoon and returned to their dressing room smiling in satisfaction.

The evening performance also went off well. By this time, Nancy felt as if she really were part of the circus. In fact, she had almost forgotten that she was only substituting for a week or so, and had to keep out of Kroon's way in order to avoid being detected.

Nevertheless, Nancy concluded that circus life was strenuous. As she was wearily removing her costume before going to bed, Erika dashed in, her eyes aglow.

"Hurry and change your clothes," she said. "We're going to have a party."

Nancy sighed, admitted she was extremely tired, and thought it best if she were excused from it.

"Oh, you have to come," Erika told her. "Lolita is giving the party and she has a surprise for you!"

"A surprise for me?" Nancy repeated.

Erika would not tell her any more. The two girls changed their clothes; then her roommate quietly led Nancy to Rancoco's trailer. Lolita and Pietro were there with several of their best friends. On a table were plates of sandwiches and bottles of soda.

"Oh, Nancy," said Lolita, hugging her, "I'm so glad you came. I don't know where to begin to tell you all that's happened in the past few hours." Then, looking at Pietro and taking his hand, she continued, "My foster father was so cruel to me today that I can't stand another minute of it. Pietro and I are eloping!"

Nancy stared, dumfounded. Then she said, "Oh, you mustn't do that!"

A hush came over the group and Nancy realized that she had thrown a damper on the gay party.

"I don't want to seem preachy," she said. "I'd better explain what I mean."

Quickly Nancy told them that during the day she had found out several things in connection with Lolita, her parents, and her foster parents. She felt it would be disastrous for the aerialist to leave at this time.

"I hate to say this," Nancy went on, "but I think Lolita, and you too, Pietro, had better stay here and watch Mr. Kroon."

Everyone in the trailer gasped. What did Nancy mean?

"I can't give you all the details," she said. "My father is going to help me. But I'll tell you this: Lolita's own mother may still be alive. And there may be some fraud in connection with money that rightfully belongs to her or Lolita. I suspect Mr. Kroon is back of it all."

Pietro came over to Nancy. He said it was he who had talked Lolita into eloping. It was impossible for him to stand by any longer and watch Kroon treat his foster daughter so cruelly.

"All he's interested in is the money her performances bring," the clown said angrily. "We could easily get jobs in another circus. Nancy, you are the one to solve the mystery. We know nothing about such things. Couldn't you find out just as much about Mr. Kroon if we weren't here?"

Nancy smiled. "I'm afraid," she said, "that if you two should leave, Kroon would become very suspicious. He might even blame me for your going away.

"I have a strong hunch that I may not fool him much longer. If he finds out I'm meddling in his affairs, he'll dismiss me at once. If that happens, I'll certainly need you here, Lolita, to help me."

Pietro threw up his hands in a gesture of resignation. "You've convinced me, Nancy," he said. Turning to Lolita, he added, "In that case, sweetheart, I'm afraid our wedding will have to be postponed."

"I guess it *is* the wise thing to do," the dainty aerialist said. "I'd much rather wait and have a happy wedding."

She thanked Nancy for persuading them to delay their plans. Then she suggested that they all eat the delicious food Rancoco's wife had supplied and enjoy the party anyway.

Early the next morning Nancy was surprised by a visit from her father. As Mr. Drew seated himself in her tent, the lawyer said he had had a hard time getting past the guard at the gate, but after he had shown the guard a permit from the local police chief, the man had let him in.

"I have a lot of news for you," he told Nancy.

"I thought it best not to give you such confidential information over the telephone."

Nancy listened intently as her father spoke. That morning River Heights Police Chief McGinnis had called and asked Mr. Drew to come down to the jail at once.

"Hitch finally made a confession," the lawyer stated. "This is the story in brief: One time while he was working with Sims' Circus, Hitch overheard Kroon accuse his wife of a kidnapping. For nearly a year the groom had blackmailed the ringmaster because of what he had heard. Then, apparently Kroon would not stand for the extortion any longer, and Hitch was thrown out.

"I'm inclined to think," Mr. Drew summarized, "that Kroon also had something on Hitch and this was the reason why the stableman never told the story before. Well, when Hitch heard that Sims' Circus was coming to River Heights, he decided to try to get back into Kroon's good graces."

As the lawyer paused, Nancy remarked, "But he wasn't able to do it?"

Her father smiled. "This will be a surprise to you. Kroon wouldn't let Hitch back into the circus, but he did carry on an intrigue with him—against you!"

"Me?" Nancy cried.

Mr. Drew nodded. He said that Hitch knew

about the bracelet with the horse charms, although he had not admitted it to Nancy. Hitch had understood that it once belonged to Lolita's mother. When he found out Nancy had it, Hitch had a good talking point with Kroon.

"He told the ringmaster what he knew and received a tidy little sum for his information. Apparently Hitch was also given the job of trying to discourage you from proceeding with your investigation. So he figured out that he would strangle you enough to give you a good scare!"

"But why did he harm poor Rosa?" Nancy asked.

Her father said that Hitch had done it in a fit of jealous rage. The stableman hated all equestrian performers because he had never succeeded in becoming a good one himself.

"And what about Señor Roberto?" Nancy questioned her father.

"Hitch insists that he had nothing to do with Roberto's injuries," Mr. Drew explained. "I believe he's telling the truth. But this only complicates matters. It's certain that Kroon didn't do it, since he was at the circus during the incident. But it does mean that there is some unknown enemy mixed up in this whole thing. I'm inclined to think he's not a member of the circus."

"But a friend of Kroon's who is helping him cheat Lolita out of her money?" Nancy asked.

Her father smiled. "I believe you've hit the nail on the head, Nancy. And this might pertain to something else that happened in River Heights. The night Hannah and I attended your first performance," the lawyer said, "your lovely horse-charm bracelet was stolen!"

CHAPTER XII

A Secret Search

THE gold bracelet with the dainty little horse charms stolen!

Nancy was upset to hear this news from her father. It had been her best clue to solving the mystery of Lolita's parents. Now she could not compare the little charms to see if the one Lolita wore was a fake.

"Don't take it so hard," Mr. Drew advised his daughter, seeing her deep frown. "I have asked Chief McGinnis to help. He'll turn up something."

Nancy told her father what the old clown Sanders had inferred about Lolita's trinket—that it was only an imitation.

"I strongly suspect," Nancy said, "that Kroon or Mrs. Kroon may have sold the original trinket and had a cheap substitute made."

"No doubt," the lawyer agreed.

"Besides wanting to solve this mystery and help Lolita," said Nancy, "I'd just love to find the sixth horse to my bracelet."

Her father smiled. "And I dare say," he remarked, "that when you do, you'll give the whole thing to Lolita Flanders for a wedding gift."

"Not unless it rightfully belongs to her," Nancy said. "After all, Aunt Eloise gave me the lovely gift, and it won't be easy to part with it."

Mr. Drew rose. "I must hurry back to River Heights, Nancy. Incidentally, Hannah and I miss you very much. We'll be glad when your week in the circus is up."

Nancy laughed. "If things go wrong here, I may be back sooner than that. By the way, Dad, have you had a chance to get in touch with anyone in England about Lola Flanders?"

Mr. Drew said that he had cabled a lawyer friend of his in London, but there had been no time for an answer.

"I'll let you know as soon as I hear anything," he promised, kissing her good-by, then leaving.

Erika came in a few moments later and at once asked what had happened to her.

"What do you mean?" Nancy asked.

"Because you look as if you'd lost your best friend."

Nancy recounted all the news Mr. Drew had given her. Erika said she was glad the mystery about Hitch had been cleared up, but she had to

admit that his story about the Kroons had compli-
cated matters.

"Do you suppose Mrs. Kroon kidnapped Lolita?" she asked, her eyes opening wide.

Nancy shrugged and asked Erika to keep the
matter in strictest confidence. If Kroon should
find out what Hitch had told the police, there
was no predicting what the ringmaster might do.

"I saw Mr. Kroon a couple of times this morning," Erika told Nancy. "He seemed to be in
worse humor than usual. Do you suppose it has
anything to do with the mystery? He might even
have found out that Lolita and Pietro had planned
to elope and then changed their minds because of
your suspicions about him."

"It's possible," said Nancy. "Pietro once remarked that there was a spy in the circus who
carries tales to Mr. Kroon."

Nancy did not tell Erika another suspicion of
hers—that the stolen bracelet might be at the
circus. She was sure that whoever had stolen it
had done so at Kroon's request.

"I must find out," the young sleuth told herself. "But how?"

Erika remarked that she hoped Nancy's concern about the mystery would not affect her
performance that afternoon. Nancy laughed and
assured Erika that she would do her best. And
she did. Later, her roommate remarked that
Nancy had never done her stunt riding better.

Nancy made a point of sitting next to Lolita at supper that evening. As soon as she had an opportunity, she asked Lolita whether she had ever mentioned her bracelet to her foster parents.

"Why, yes, I did. Is something the matter?"

Nancy did not reply, but asked Lolita if she could remember when this was. The aerialist thought a few moments, then said it was sometime during the last day that the circus was in River Heights.

There was no question now in Nancy's mind that Kroon had engineered the theft. During the rest of the meal, she kept trying to figure out how to prove it.

"I'll bet whoever stole the bracelet brought it here to the circus," she reasoned. "And if he did, it's my guess that the bracelet is hidden in Mr. Kroon's trailer."

Later, Nancy told Dan Webster about the theft of the bracelet and why she thought it might be in Kroon's possession. She said she wondered how she could find out whether her suspicions were correct.

"I thought perhaps I'd get in touch with the police captain," she said. "Maybe he could make a search."

Dan Webster agreed that this was the sensible thing to do, but it had one big drawback.

"Kroon will know at once that you instigated the search, since it's your bracelet," he reminded

Nancy. "He'll instantly make trouble for you, Lolita, and the other riders."

Nancy admitted that there was merit in Dan Webster's objections. Suddenly her eyes lighted up.

"Dan," she said, "how would you like to play detective for me?"

"Me?" Dan Webster began to laugh. "You don't mean you want me to make the search. I'd be sure to get caught."

"No, not to make the search. Just lay the groundwork for me," Nancy suggested.

Dan Webster scratched his head. "Well, keep talking. I'll let you know my answer after I hear what you want me to do."

"I can't tell you now," Nancy said hurriedly. "I see Mr. Kroon coming. I'll meet you in your office after the show."

The two separated, but after the performance was over, Nancy returned to Webster's office. She said to the horse trainer in a low voice.

"This is what I'd like you to do. First, follow Mr. Kroon until he goes to his trailer. Then call on him."

"But what excuse could I use?" Dan Webster asked.

"Oh, that's easy," Nancy said quickly. "Tell him that Rosa will not be able to perform by the end of the week. Ask him what he thinks about letting the new girl continue a while longer."

"But how is this going to help you find your bracelet?" the horse trainer questioned, puzzled.

"Dan," Nancy went on, "tell him that you've heard rumors of things disappearing from the circus. Watch Mr. Kroon's face intently to see if there's any change of expression or if the ringmaster's eyes dart to some possible hiding place. Then tell him you've heard that someone is going to ask for a police search unless a valuable piece of jewelry that was stolen from her turns up."

As Nancy gave her instructions, Dan Webster sat gazing at the floor. He shook his head several times but did not speak. Finally he looked up.

"Nancy, dear," he said, "I want to help you as much as I can. But this is a big order. I'm afraid I'd fail. You'd better count me out and get somebody else."

Nancy laughed softly. "Oh, it isn't that bad, Dan," she told him. "I'll tell you what. Suppose I stand outside the window and watch Kroon's actions. You pretend to know nothing about what's going on, but try to follow the lines of conversation I suggested."

At last, Dan Webster said he would attempt it, and the time was set for eleven thirty. Nancy thanked him and hurried off to change her clothes. When Erika saw her starting out again, she asked Nancy where she was going.

"To do some sleuthing. But don't be worried. I'm not going to leave the circus grounds."

Nancy hurried from the tent. Using a circuitous route to avoid as many people as possible, she went to Mr. Kroon's trailer. She could hear voices inside distinctly.

No one was in sight. Nancy cautiously crept to the side window and stood on a box. Through the window she could see the interior and remain out of the line of vision of those within.

Dan Webster was there, talking with Lolita's foster parents. Evidently the early part of the previously planned conversation had already taken place, because Kroon was just saying, "The new girl's all right, but I'll let you know tomorrow about her staying with us after this week. There are certain things about her I don't like."

"What are they?" Dan asked quickly.

"Nothing that you could do anything about, Webster," the ringmaster replied. "They're personal reasons."

Dan rose, but before leaving he said, "By the way, Mr. Kroon, I've heard rumors about things disappearing from the circus."

Kroon gave a slight twitch, and Nancy saw his eyes travel involuntarily to a bureau in the trailer.

To Dan he said, "I haven't heard anything about it. You shouldn't believe everything you hear."

"Probably not," Dan Webster gave a slightly forced laugh. "I guess rumors fly around thick and fast in the circus."

He left the trailer and started for his own quarters. Dan had failed to carry out the last part of Nancy's instructions, but it did not matter. She had found out what she wanted to know.

The bureau was probably the hiding place!

Nancy continued to eavesdrop outside the trailer, but neither Mr. nor Mrs. Kroon mentioned the bracelet or Dan's visit.

Presently Mrs. Kroon went to Lolita's trailer, apparently to watch her foster daughter's movements.

A few minutes later the window shades on both trailers were drawn and soon afterward the lights were turned off. Nancy returned to her tent, convinced that her bracelet was in the bureau in Kroon's trailer. She hoped that the ringmaster would not remove it before she had a chance to carry out the next part of her plan.

Early the following morning she went to find Lolita. She was forced to wait for several minutes while the aerialist and her foster parents finished breakfast in Mr. and Mrs. Kroon's trailer. Finally the ringmaster left, and Lolita started back to her own quarters.

Nancy signaled her to walk to a more secluded spot where they might talk. Quickly she divulged her suspicions about the bracelet. Lolita was aghast to learn that her foster father might be a thief. Nancy said she was sorry but felt that it was necessary for Lolita to know all the facts.

"I want you to search that bureau," Nancy told her.

Lolita looked frightened. "But how can I?" she said. "Mother's always in one trailer or the other."

"I'll arrange for her to leave," said Nancy. "I'll have Erika ask her to come to our tent and help with some sewing."

Lolita finally consented. An hour later, when Mrs. Kroon was safely out of the way, the aerialist went into her father's trailer. Nancy posted herself at the window. Some distance away was Dan Webster, acting as a lookout.

Lolita pulled out drawer after drawer, lifting various articles and feeling beneath pieces of clothing. The bracelet was not in any of the drawers. Just as Lolita opened the lowest drawer, Nancy heard a low whistle. Looking up, she saw Dan Webster warning her of danger.

Reinhold Kroon was almost at the trailer!

Through the window Nancy hissed at Lolita. The girl was so engrossed in her search that she did not hear her friend. The next moment, Kroon stepped inside.

CHAPTER XIII

Blackout

WHEN Lolita heard someone step into the trailer, she slammed the bureau drawer shut. But her movement and the telltale clothes hanging from the drawer gave her away.

"Answer me! What are you doing?" her foster father yelled.

He took hold of the girl's arm and yanked her around violently. "You tell me what you were doing or I'll——" The ringmaster did not finish because of an unexpected interruption.

Fearful that Lolita might give away their secret, Nancy acted quickly. She had once learned a few ventriloquistic tricks. Using one of them now, she threw her voice to sound as if it were inside the trailer and gave an unearthly scream. Then, dashing around to the door of the trailer, she ran inside.

"I heard a scream," she said. "Is something the matter?"

Kroon glared at Nancy and released his hold on Lolita. The pretty aerialist sagged weakly onto a couch.

"Oh, Nancy!" she wailed helplessly.

Kroon's eyes narrowed and he walked toward Nancy menacingly. "Why, you little double-crosser!" he shouted.

Nancy stood her ground. Out of the corner of her eye she could see Dan Webster in the doorway. Should she need any protection, it was nearby.

"Nancy, eh?" the ringmaster yelled. "You're Nancy Drew, that self-styled detective, and you sneaked in here to spy on the circus!"

Nancy said nothing. This seemed to infuriate the man. Towering above her, he waved a finger in her face.

"I knew you'd joined the circus and I let you stay because you were a good rider," he raved. "But I've had spies trailing you. Don't think you've put anything over on me, you little sneak!"

"Nancy has done nothing wrong," Lolita said stanchly. "She's performed beautifully in this circus."

"Is that so?" Kroon said harshly. "I suppose you were snooping through this bureau because Nancy Drew told you to. What were you looking for?"

"Why, you little double-crosser!" the ringmaster shouted.

Lolita turned pleadingly to Nancy. She did not know how to answer.

Nancy decided to speak. "What's so terrible about your daughter's looking through your bureau? Goodness, whenever I want a big hanky I go to my father's chest of drawers."

Kroon was not fooled by Nancy's play acting. At the top of his lungs, he shouted, "You get out of this circus and stay out!"

"What about the Vascons' act?" Lolita cried.

The ringmaster said that Rosa would perform that afternoon or the whole troupe could leave the circus. In no case was Nancy Drew to appear. She was to leave the grounds at once.

In the doorway Dan Webster could remain silent no longer. Stepping inside, he pleaded for Nancy to remain. Kroon would not listen.

Seeing that it was useless to argue with him, Nancy looked straight at Kroon and said, "I'll go but not until you give me back my bracelet!"

Kroon gave a slight start but instantly recovered his poise. "What are you talking about?" he bellowed.

"I'm talking about a gold bracelet with horse charms. It was stolen from my house and I have good reason to believe that you have it."

Kroon's eyes blazed. He said that he ought to have Nancy arrested for defamation of character. It was only because of her youth that he would not prosecute.

"Now get out of here, all of you!" he yelled, shoving them through the doorway. He followed the others outside, then slammed and locked the door.

"Lolita," he said, "go to your quarters. And if you ever dare to communicate with Nancy Drew again, I'll punish you in a way you won't forget."

The ringmaster strode away. Lolita, ill from fright, hurried off to her own trailer. Nancy felt it best not to follow.

She walked off with Dan Webster, who asked her if she were willing to take a chance and remain with the circus. Surprised, the young sleuth remarked that this would hardly be safe.

"I'd hate to see the Vascons fired," Dan said. "But I'm afraid that's what will happen. I dropped into the doctor's this morning. He said Rosa would not be able to stunt ride for at least a couple of weeks.

"If you could just finish out the week, I'm sure we can find another substitute rider by that time," Dan pleaded.

Nancy said she was willing if she could possibly get away with the subterfuge. It would give her a chance to learn more about what was going on in the circus. On the spur of the moment she thought of a plan.

"Suppose I room with someone else in the circus," she said. "Rosa can move back to Erika's tent. Since Mr. Kroon probably will be watching, Rosa might dress and ride in the parade. Then, when it's time for her act, I'll substitute for her."

Dan Webster smiled. "We'll do it! I'll arrange for you to stay in the hospital tent. Kroon would never think of looking for you there." He winked. "Besides, the doc and his nurse are good friends of mine."

Nancy now told the horse trainer that she was afraid Kroon might return to his trailer and take the bracelet away. She did not want this to happen and she asked if Dan Webster could possibly help her again.

"You did very well the last time you became a sleuth," she encouraged him.

The horse trainer laughed and said that he did not believe he could get away with it a second time. Kroon would be sure to know something was up. Dan suggested that one of his midget friends act as lookout.

"Little Will can be trusted implicitly," he said.

Nancy knew the pleasant man and consented to the plan. Then she told Dan that she was going to telephone her friends Bess and George in River Heights and ask them to drive to Danford.

"Kroon may discover our plan," she said. "In that case, I'll need transportation home. Besides, the girls can relieve Little Will in watching Mr. Kroon's trailer."

A few minutes later Nancy telephoned George, who promised that she and Bess would start immediately for Danford.

"I'll be hiding in the hospital tent, George. Come there."

The cousins arrived shortly before the afternoon performance. Bess was aghast to hear what had been happening and tried her best to coax Nancy to go home with her and George at once. But the girl detective contended that it was important to stay.

Just before parade time, Dan Webster came to tell Nancy that Little Will had watched the trailer constantly. Mrs. Kroon had entered it directly after luncheon and had not come out since.

"How would it be if I relieve your midget friend now?" George proposed.

Nancy thought this was a good idea. George went off, and Bess remained with Nancy. She would act as a messenger, carrying the riding costume back and forth.

Presently the gong sounded for the parade to begin. Rosa, seated on the beautiful horse, took her position, and Nancy watched from a nearby place of concealment. As the girl detective had predicted, Kroon was on hand to meet her. He smiled in satisfaction.

Apparently convinced that his orders were being carried out, the ringmaster did not stay in the tent after he introduced the Vascon troupe. Nancy felt a little nervous but she did her part well.

When the act was over, Nancy quickly ran to the hospital tent. She removed her costume and Bess hurried with it to Rosa. She returned in a few minutes and reported that her cousin was still on duty. Little Will had gone to eat his supper, then would take George's place until he had to perform again.

Three supper trays were brought in, and Nancy and Bess began to eat.

"Nancy, why don't you turn this case over to the police?" Bess suggested.

Nancy said she hated to do so without more evidence.

"But you can't keep up this watching and performing. You'll need sleep," Bess argued. "And George and I can't help you much longer. We'll have to start home in a little while."

"Oh, please stay overnight," Nancy begged. "By tomorrow I'm sure we'll find out about the bracelet. Won't you call home and tell your mother and George's that you'll be here?"

Bess finally agreed and made the call. George arrived in a few minutes to eat her supper. She had left Little Will on guard. Kroon had not entered the trailer and Mrs. Kroon had not left it.

The evening performance closed without arousing the ringmaster's suspicions that Nancy had been pinch-hitting for Rosa. Relieved, Nancy had just reached the hospital tent when George rushed in.

"Nancy! News!" she cried.

Breathlessly, she told Nancy that Kroon had sneaked up to the trailer from the rear shortly after the evening performance had begun. Mrs. Kroon had handed him a small package through the window. The ringmaster had then given it to the son of one of the aerialists and told him to mail it.

"I followed the boy toward the post office," George went on. "As we got under a light, I pretended to bump into him. When he dropped the package, I read the address on it. And listen to this! It was going to Lola Flanders, care of Tristam Booking Agency in New York City!"

"Oh, George, you're wonderful!" Nancy cried gleefully. "We'll call the local police and have them get in touch with the New York police. They'll be able to investigate the package and the booking agency and maybe find Mrs. Flanders!"

The excited girls raced from the tent and over to the telephone booth. George waited outside while Nancy stepped in to make the call. She picked up the receiver and put in a coin. When there was no response, Nancy realized the telephone was out of order.

"I'll have to go down to headquarters," she decided.

Opening the door of the booth, Nancy looked around. George was not there. The next instant a thick dark cloth was thrown over Nancy's head. She struggled, but it was useless. Suddenly she blacked out!

CHAPTER XIV

George's Discovery

NANCY became aware of the rumble and harsh clatter of wheels. At first it seemed far away, then it grew louder and louder.

Slowly she opened her eyes but could see nothing. Her brain was foggy and she had no idea where she was. As her mind cleared, Nancy realized she was bound and gagged.

"Oh, yes," she recalled. "When I came out of that telephone booth, someone put a cloth over my head and I blacked out."

Nancy now realized that she was in a moving vehicle. The steady rhythm of the wheels told her that she was on a train. Was it a sleeping compartment?

"Probably not," Nancy decided. "I'm lying on the floor. I must be in a freight car."

As her strength returned, she tried to get out

of her bonds, but her struggles were futile. Whoever had tied the knots had done a good job.

"Oh, if I could only remove this gag!"

Nancy tried rubbing her cheek against the floor to accomplish this, but again her efforts were unsuccessful. There was not a sound within the car and Nancy decided that she was alone. While she was wondering where the freight train was going and how long a trip it might be, she heard a muffled sound from someone not far away from her. Nancy shuddered. Was this person a guard?

Once more she tried to loosen the ropes that bound her arms and legs. She managed to slide them an inch, but they still remained tightly around her.

As Nancy got over her fright, it occurred to her that the other person in the car might be a prisoner as well. George disappeared rather mysteriously. Could she be the person who had made the sound?

Nancy wriggled toward the direction from which the sound had come. Finding the other person's hand, she squirmed. It was cold and unresponsive. But upon investigation, she was convinced of one thing: it was a girl's hand.

Inching herself upward, Nancy's hand came to a rope. The other person was bound too!

Moving still farther along the floor, Nancy felt the girl's face. There was a gag over it, but by twisting and turning, Nancy managed, after some difficulty, to loosen the knot and remove the gag.

Nancy ran her fingers over the girl's features and came to the conclusion that she was indeed George Fayne. She mumbled as loudly as she could, "George! George! Wake up!"

Presently the girl stirred, and Nancy's heart leaped in relief. After muttering some unintelligible words, George finally said, "Where am I?"

"Oh, George, I'm so glad you've awakened," Nancy mumbled.

"Nancy, where are we? What happened?"

The girl detective replied that they were in a freight car. Where the train was going, she had no idea—it might be heading for the coast.

"But we're going to get out of here," she said with determination. "George, can you turn on your side? I'll try to loosen these ropes, then you can do the same for me."

"You must have a gag over your mouth," said George. "Your voice sounds so different."

"I have," said Nancy. "See if you can get it off." She turned her face away from George, and after several futile attempts, George finally loosened the gag.

"That's better. Thanks a lot," Nancy said. "Now I'll unfasten your ropes."

George turned on her side and Nancy felt for the knots. Untying them was slow work. Her hands ached from the effort.

George, freed, suggested that she untie Nancy's hands before freeing her own legs. She felt for the knots. Upon finding the first one, she began the difficult task of loosening it.

"I've never met a more stubborn knot in my life," she said.

But she persevered and at last was rewarded. Two other ropes bound Nancy's arms, and it was twenty minutes before George was able to get them off.

"Oh, that feels wonderful!" Nancy said. "Now to get these ropes off our legs."

As George struggled with hers, she remarked, "It will be twenty-five miles more before I get these untied."

The process did take a long time, and while the girls were at it, they began to discuss what had happened to them.

"I guess I'm responsible for all this," said George. "That boy who took the package to the post office possibly told Mr. Kroon what happened the minute he got back to the circus."

Nancy agreed and added, "He wanted to make sure that we didn't communicate with the police before he had a chance to retrieve the package."

"You mean he'll try to get it from the post office?"

Nancy said that she did not think the ringmaster would dare attempt that. But he probably did plan to keep George and Nancy prisoners until the package could reach New York and be delivered.

"But this is where my work to stop him begins," she said resolutely. "Here goes the last knot."

Within a few minutes George also was free.

"After being in this darkness so long," said George, "my other senses seem to be keener. I'll bet I can walk right to the side door of this freight car."

She was about to try when the freight went around a curve and she was thrown to the floor. After the train was once more on the straightaway, both girls made their way to the side of the car. The door and the mechanism that opened it were easy to find. But try as they might, they could not budge the door an inch.

"It's probably locked from the outside," Nancy decided.

"Then we're stuck," George said in disgust. "Hypers, Nancy, we've got to get out of here before someone comes along and captures us again."

Nancy concurred.

Suddenly George had an idea. "Maybe there's a hatch in the roof of this car," she said.

"I doubt it," Nancy answered. "Only old refrigerator cars have them. But I'll be glad to find out. Do you think you can hold me on your shoulders while I investigate the roof?"

"Sure."

George leaned over and Nancy climbed onto her shoulders. But trying to stand up straight and balance herself in the swaying car was even more difficult than standing on a cantering horse. Twice she had to jump off to avoid pitching headlong, and once she just missed crashing into the side of the freight car.

At last Nancy was able to stand on George's shoulders and reach up to the roof of the car. After feeling around for several minutes, she concluded that there was no hatch and jumped down.

"George," she said, "we never thought of a door on the other side of this car."

Annoyed at themselves, they hurried to find out. Their fingers found a latch! The girls hardly dared hope the door would be unlocked, but as they pulled on it, the sliding panel moved!

"Thank goodness!" George cried. "Now we can get out of this prison."

"Not yet," Nancy told her, as she saw the scenery flashing past them. "We're traveling at about fifty miles an hour."

She guessed at the time. It must be an hour or so after dawn.

"Where do you suppose we are?" George asked.

Cultivated fields stretched on every side, but there was not a house in sight.

"I wonder what the chances are of the freight slowing down," said Nancy.

"Now we can get out of this prison," George cried.

As if in answer to her wish, the train reached a long uphill grade and began to lose speed. In a short time it was moving very slowly.

A few minutes later the freight train was moving at about five miles an hour. The two girls selected a favorable spot and jumped from the slowly moving train. They were free!

Nancy and George started rapidly across a field before anyone on the freight train might become aware of their presence. A quarter of a mile farther on, they reached a road.

"Oh, hurray! There's a farmhouse!" George cried. "I never was so glad to see a house in my life!"

Nancy grinned. She was delighted herself. At the farmhouse they found an elderly couple. They looked searchingly at the girls' disheveled appearance when Nancy asked to use their telephone.

"I guess so," the man answered. "Where you two be comin' from this early hour of the mornin'?"

"Why—uh—we were out riding," Nancy replied haltingly. "We—uh—left our car over by the railroad."

"Broke down, eh?" the man said, as he led her to the telephone.

Nancy put in a call to her home, reversing the charges. It hardly seemed as if the telephone had started to ring when Hannah answered. The frantic woman wanted to know if Nancy was all right.

"I'm fine, Hannah," she said. "Don't worry about me. I'll be home after a while."

"Where are you?" the housekeeper asked.

"Just a minute. I'll find out."

Nancy turned to the man and asked where she was. He said they were not far from the town of Black River. The girl relayed this to Hannah.

"My goodness," she said, "that's about a hundred miles from here."

Nancy said that if she needed any assistance getting home she would call again. She asked the housekeeper to notify George's parents that their daughter was with her and was all right.

After she had completed the telephone call, Nancy asked the farmer if it would be possible for him to drive the girls to town.

"I'll be glad to," he said. "I was going anyway, just as soon as I have my breakfast. Have you eaten yet?"

When they said no, the farmer's wife invited the callers to join them.

During the meal, the kindly couple were curious to learn more about their visitors, but the girls were wary of saying anything.

Upon arriving in Black River, the pair immediately went to the State Police Office, gave their names, and explained what had happened to them.

"We haven't a shred of evidence to prove who was responsible," said Nancy, "only suspicions. And the police are already working on the case, so I'm not asking your help except to get us home. We haven't a penny with us."

"I can do that," the officer said, smiling. He took some money from a drawer and handed it to Nancy. "Return the cash when it's convenient."

The girls thanked him and went to the bus station. A short time later they boarded a bus to River Heights and reached home at nine o'clock.

Mr. Drew hugged his daughter, and Hannah wiped away tears of joy. After the greetings and explanations were over, Nancy said ruefully, "I won't dare go back to Sims' Circus, I suppose. I wonder what will happen to the Vascons' act."

"That's no longer your worry, Nancy," her father said firmly. "What's more, you're leaving town at once. Let Kroon think his diabolical plan was a success."

"Where am I going?" Nancy asked.

"How would you like to visit Aunt Eloise and continue to work on the case in New York?" he suggested.

Nancy kissed her father. "Dad, you're a genius. I can't think of anything I'd rather do!"

CHAPTER XV

New York Yields a Lead

As Nancy quickly packed her bags in order to catch the afternoon plane to New York, she discussed further angles of the case with her father.

"Don't you think George ought to go away, too?" she asked.

"Yes, I do," her father replied. "Why don't you ask her to join you?"

Nancy telephoned her friend and learned that the Faynes were taking George on a motor trip.

Nancy's next call was to Bess. It had been she who had discovered that Nancy and George had disappeared from the circus. Bess had summoned Mr. Drew, who had gone at once to question Kroon. The ringmaster had told the lawyer he had discharged Nancy because she was not a regular member of the circus. He had assumed that Nancy, of course, had gone home.

"Kroon is slick," Mr. Drew said, "but I don't think he'll suspect that you've gone to New York."

Mr. Drew drove his daughter to the airport and waved good-by as she boarded the plane. Nancy settled herself and promptly fell asleep from exhaustion. She arrived in New York refreshed and ready to continue work.

Nancy took a taxi to Eloise Drew's apartment and soon the two were embracing each other.

"How good it is to see you!" Miss Drew exclaimed.

"You're a dear to let me barge in like this," Nancy said. "Aunt Eloise, how in the world did you get that picture of me?"

Nancy's eyes focused on a large photograph on a table. She was in her circus costume, standing on a horse.

Miss Drew laughed. "I asked a photographer at the circus to take it when I was there," she said. "It came out very well, don't you think?"

While Nancy and her aunt ate supper, the conversation turned to the mystery. Nancy told Miss Drew that her father had given her a letter of introduction from Police Chief McGinnis to Captain Smith of the New York Police Department, who had been assigned to the Tristam Booking Agency investigation.

"First thing tomorrow morning I'm going down to talk to Captain Smith," she said. "I wonder what he found out about Lola Flanders. Wouldn't it be wonderful if she really were Lolita's mother?"

Aunt Eloise was not so sure of this. Perhaps the woman had changed in the last ten years. It was very strange that she had not been in touch with her daughter.

"At least Lolita knows nothing about this," Nancy replied. "If it seems best not to tell her, I'll keep it a secret."

Directly after breakfast the next morning Nancy set off for Captain Smith's headquarters. She presented the letter of introduction to the sergeant on duty, who took it to the captain. In a moment the sergeant returned and ushered Nancy into the captain's office.

"I'm glad to meet you, Miss Drew," the officer said, smiling. "Chief McGinnis and I were buddies in the Army some years ago. He tells me that you're quite a detective."

Nancy blushed and admitted that she had solved some cases. Then she turned the conversation from herself and asked, "Have you found Lola Flanders?"

Captain Smith told her that one of their detectives had called at the Tristam Booking Agency. He found that Lola Flanders was a young dancer who used the stage name of Millie Francine.

"A young dancer!" Nancy repeated. "Then this

Lola Flanders is not the person I'm looking for."

Nancy thought a few moments. Could this young Lola Flanders be a relative of Lolita's?

"Where is the dancer now?" Nancy asked the police captain.

"She's working here in New York," he replied. "I've checked. The story is correct."

The captain said that the police were watching the mails. The package from Danford had not yet arrived. As soon as it did, it would be impounded and X-rayed.

"If you'll leave your telephone number, I'll call you as soon as the package has been examined."

Nancy returned to her aunt's apartment. Just before noon, Captain Smith telephoned. "The package is here," he said. "Can you come over?"

"I'll be there!" Nancy cried.

When she reached Captain Smith's office, he pointed to a bracelet lying on his desk. "Is that yours?" he asked.

At first glance Nancy thought it was, but when she examined it, she changed her mind. This bracelet had six horses and the gold was much darker than hers had been.

"I'm afraid it isn't mine," Nancy said, considerably embarrassed. She told him why.

Captain Smith took the bracelet to the window and looked at it in the strong light.

"I'm no expert at judging jewelry," he said,

"but this bracelet may have been tampered with to change its appearance."

"May I use your telephone to call Chief McGinnis?" Nancy asked. "I'd like him to check with the girl at the circus who has a horse charm similar to these."

"Go ahead," the captain said.

Upon hearing Nancy's story, Chief McGinnis promised to get in touch with the police in the town where the circus was now playing.

"I'll call Captain Smith as soon as I have the answer," he said.

Shortly after lunch Captain Smith called Nancy at her aunt's apartment to report that Lolita still had her horse charm.

"Captain Smith," Nancy said, "will you go with me and my aunt to the shop where she purchased the bracelet? The owner should be able to identify the one you're holding if it is the original."

The officer said he would meet them at the shop in twenty minutes. At the appointed time the three walked into the shop. After hearing their story, Mr. Abrams, the owner, examined the bracelet. Using a special powder and a piece of chamois, he began to rub the jewelry. In a few minutes the gold was shining again.

"Yes, this is the bracelet I sold Miss Drew," Mr. Abrams said. "Whoever put this sixth charm on was an amateur. It is a bad job."

Nancy's thoughts flew at once to Mr. and Mrs.

Kroon. Had the woman attached it and wrapped the bracelet for mailing while George and Little Will had been watching the trailer? Had the Kroons stolen the original charm from Lolita's necklace some time ago and kept it, hoping to locate the valuable bracelet, attach the missing horse, and sell the jewelry at a high price?

"Mr. Abrams," said Nancy, "can you tell from your records where you purchased the bracelet?"

"In just a minute," the shop owner said. He went into a back room but returned presently and handed Nancy a piece of paper.

"I got the bracelet from a London pawn-broker," he said. "Here is the name and address."

Nancy thanked Mr. Abrams for his help and left the shop with her aunt. Captain Smith handed Nancy the bracelet. She thanked him and then asked if he could find out from London who had signed the pawn ticket.

"Certainly," Captain Smith said. "I can do it through the London police. It will take a while but I'll call you when I hear."

The following morning at about eleven o'clock he phoned. "It begins to look as if you're getting somewhere, Miss Drew," he said. "The pawn ticket was signed with a nervous scrawl that was hardly legible. It looks like Laura Flynn."

"It could be Lola Flanders!" Nancy cried.

"It's possible," the captain agreed. "The ticket

was signed three years ago. The shop keeps things for only two years, then sells them."

After saying good-by, Nancy thought about this latest news. Suddenly her eyes began to sparkle. She dialed her father's office. When he answered she told him of her discovery.

Then she said, "Dad, will you fly to London with me right away?"

"What!" Mr. Drew exclaimed. "Fly to London?"

"That's right, Dad. You need a vacation and you can help me solve this mystery. Who knows, we may find Lolita's mother and bring her back with us."

The lawyer laughed. "You're very persuasive. All right, Nancy. We'll go."

"Oh, Dad, you're a sweetheart!" Nancy cried. "When can you get here?"

"I might as well leave right now," he said. "I'll catch the night plane. You see if you can get reservations for tomorrow."

"I'll call you back," Nancy said. "In the meantime, can you find out if there have been any new developments in Sims' Circus?"

"Bess called here a little while ago," Nancy's father said. "Lolita had been in touch with her. Kroon has dismissed Pietro and no one knows where he has gone."

"That is bad news," Nancy remarked.

When her father said good-by, Nancy called the airline and reserved seats on a plane leaving late the next afternoon. She then called her father and gave him the good news.

"I'm looking forward to a trip with you, Nancy," he said, "but I can't have you to myself until we're on the plane. Ned is coming with me to see us off. By the way, I'll bring your passport."

Nancy and her aunt rose early to meet the plane from River Heights. To their amazement, not only did Mr. Drew and Ned step off the airliner, but Pietro as well.

"It's good to see you, Pietro!" Nancy cried.

Pietro explained that he was going to London to see his father and had a reservation on the same plane as the Drews.

After he had been introduced to Aunt Eloise, the group found a taxi and drove to Miss Drew's apartment. With the excuse that he had some shopping to do, Ned asked Nancy to go out with him until it was time to leave for the airport.

While they were having lunch in a cozy restaurant, Ned suddenly warned Nancy not to get any crazy ideas about staying in England.

"Why, Ned," she said, "what a funny thing to say!"

"Well, I understand Pietro is planning to stay."

Then Nancy caught on. She started to laugh. "Why, Ned Nickerson!" she said. "Just because Kroon told Lolita she couldn't marry Pietro, there's no reason to think he wants to marry me!"

"I'm not so sure," Ned replied glumly.

"Don't be silly," said Nancy sternly. "I'll come back just as soon as I can find out something about Lola Flanders."

Ned looked relieved.

When they reached the apartment again, Nancy telephoned Captain Smith to ask if any more had been learned about the Tristam Booking Agency.

"We have rather important information," the officer reported. "Our men have been watching Lola Flanders' mail. She has been receiving a great number of what look like dividend checks."

Nancy told the captain that she was flying to London and would get in touch with him when she returned.

"Perhaps I'll have learned more for you by that time," Captain Smith said as he hung up.

Nancy discussed these latest findings with her father. It seemed to her that Reinhold Kroon was using the agency as a coverup. He was stealing money that belonged to the real Lola Flanders, using Millie Francine as a front.

Mr. Drew agreed that this might be the case. "Perhaps the police will have the answer by the time we return," he said. "We'd better start for the airport now."

An hour later the Drews and Pietro checked in at the ticket counter. They each had a large suitcase for the baggage compartment and a small overnight bag to carry. While waiting for the signal to board the plane Nancy walked down to the end of the long room to examine a map on the wall.

She was tracing the course of their flight across the Atlantic when out of the corner of her eye she saw a man pick up her overnight case and run off with it.

"Stop!" Nancy called, dashing after him.

Holding the case in front of him, the man ran on. As Nancy drew closer to him, she thought he was trying to open the unlocked bag. Why?

"Stop, thief!" Nancy shouted.

This time the man dropped the bag and fled down a nearby stairway. Nancy picked up the bag and noticed a corner of her pink-flowered robe protruding from it.

"He did open it!" she thought in surprise. The woman's lounge was close by. Nancy hurried in and sat down in a chair with the bag on her lap. She opened it wide.

Acrid fumes poured from the case. An open bottle lay among the disarranged toilet articles.

Nancy began to cough and choke. The next moment the fumes reached her eyes.

"I can't see!" Nancy cried in alarm.

CHAPTER XVI

A Lucky Hunch

AT Nancy's outcry, the attendant rushed forward. "What's the trouble, miss?" she asked.

"My eyes!" Nancy groaned. "Someone put acid in my bag. Please help me!"

The frightened attendant said she would take Nancy to the first-aid station. Guiding the stricken girl through the waiting room with one hand and carrying her bag in the other, the woman led Nancy to the airport infirmary. A nurse hurried forward to take charge.

Nancy quickly explained what had happened, and at once she and her bag were taken into the doctor's office.

The odor of the fumes was very evident and the doctor recognized them at once. He took down a bottle of oily liquid and some gauze sponges from a shelf. Soaking a sponge, he dabbed it on her eyes.

"Take that bag out into the fresh air!" he ordered.

The nurse hurriedly went off with it, while the doctor continued to swab Nancy's eyes. Presently she was able to see dimly.

"You're lucky," the physician said. "If that acid had spilled in your eyes, you would have become blind. But the fumes only affected them for a short time."

By now Nancy was able to see clearly again. She thanked the doctor for his prompt help.

"I'm glad I was here," he said, smiling. Then he sobered. "Would you mind telling me why you were carrying that deadly acid with you?"

When Nancy told him her story, the man's eyebrows raised in amazement. "I'll report this to the police at once," he declared.

Back in the large waiting room, Mr. Drew and his companions wondered what had happened to Nancy.

"She probably went to telephone again," Ned said.

"Well, I wish she'd hurry," Mr. Drew remarked. "We'll be taking off in a few minutes."

Ned had been staring at an unusual sight, just outside the window. A woman's overnight bag lay open on the ground. A white-uniformed nurse and a policeman were carefully examining its contents.

Ned laughed and pointed out the scene to Miss

Drew. "That has all the earmarks of a mystery," he said. "Nancy is missing it."

"Why, that looks like Nancy's robe," she said. "I wonder what could have happened?"

The whole group hurried outside to the policeman and inquired what the trouble was. Impatiently, he replied, "Some fool girl was carrying a bottle of acid in her bag. It came uncorked. The doctor is taking care of her."

"What!" Mr. Drew cried. Turning to the nurse, he said he was the girl's father. "Please take us to her at once."

Reaching the infirmary, they burst into the doctor's office. "Nancy! What happened?" Mr. Drew cried.

Quickly she gave him the details.

"The fiend!" Pietro cried. "I'll stay here and find that fellow if it's the last thing I do!"

"That won't be necessary," said Mr. Drew. "The police can take care of him."

The doctor said Nancy was able to travel, so she went outside with the others. She could give the policeman only a hazy description of the man who had taken her bag since she had not seen more than his back.

Nancy looked in dismay at her suitcase. The acid had spilled on some of the clothing, and it was ruined. Luckily it had not damaged the bag itself, and Nancy was able to retrieve some of her belongings.

Over the loudspeaker came the announcement: "Flight two-oh-five departing for London!"

Pietro and the Drews said good-by and walked toward the plane. A few minutes later the pilot taxied down the runway, then with a roar the huge plane rose into the sky.

Nancy watched from the window as long as land was in sight. Then, as the plane went higher and higher into the clouds, she settled down to read the magazine Aunt Eloise had given her.

After a delicious dinner and a long nap, Nancy realized the plane was descending. The FASTEN SEAT BELTS sign flashed on. They were over London!

When they landed, Nancy and her companions were among the first to leave the plane. After going through Customs, they walked toward the exit gate. Pietro saw his father and started to run.

Nancy enjoyed watching the happy reunion as the two men embraced. When the Drews walked up, Pietro introduced them to his father, Mr. Favia.

"This is the young lady I wrote you about," the clown said, "the one who is trying to straighten out everything so that Lolita and I can be married."

"Then I am doubly glad to meet you, Miss Drew," the older man said, smiling.

"And I'm happy to meet you," said Nancy. "You know you're involved in this mystery. It is because you thought you saw Lola Flanders at the circus in Tewkesbury that we're here."

"I've made reservations for my son and myself at a small West End hotel. Now that you are here, I am sure they could take care of you and your father too."

Mr. Drew agreed, and they took a taxi. Pietro told his father what had happened to Nancy at the New York airport. A worried look came over the older man's face and he said he hoped she would have no such experiences in England.

"I'm sure I'll be all right," Nancy said. "But you men will have to let me do a little shopping. That awful man and his acid ruined some rather necessary articles in my wardrobe."

After breakfast, the group set off for the shopping trip and a visit to the pawnshop from which Nancy's bracelet had come. When they reached Liberty's Department Store, Mr. Drew suggested Nancy be given half an hour for her shopping.

"We men will look around and meet you here," he said, as he handed her some English money.

Hurrying from one counter to another, Nancy made several purchases.

"I ought to pick up a few souvenirs while I'm here," she told herself. "I must get something for Aunt Eloise and Hannah. And for George and Bess. They were wonderful, helping me on the mystery."

Nancy had so much fun buying some of the

lovely things for which the store was famous that she actually forgot the time. When she rejoined her companions, she apologized for keeping them waiting.

"You did pretty well at that," her father teased. "Most girls would have taken half a day to buy all those things," he said, looking at her many packages.

The pawnshop was not far away. The owner proved to be very helpful. Although it had been three years since the woman who had signed her name as Laura Flynn had visited his shop, he remembered her well.

"I felt sorry for her," he said. "She seemed very nervous. Apparently it was hard for her to part with the bracelet." When he described her, Nancy was at once reminded of Lolita.

"She's the one I saw in Tewkesbury, all right!" Mr. Favia exclaimed.

Nancy wanted to start at once to look for Lola Flanders. But the others insisted that she should do some sightseeing in London first. Mr. Drew wanted to call on his lawyer friend, so Pietro and his father showed Nancy the most famous sights of the old city.

The next morning Mr. Drew hired a comfortable car to use during their stay in England. They set out early with Pietro's father behind the wheel.

Nancy was charmed with the countryside as

they approached the town of Tewkesbury. Presently Mr. Favia asked her where she intended to search. He had already made inquiries in several places.

"I have an idea that Lola Flanders may be in a nursing home of some sort," Nancy said.

"That's a good hunch," her father remarked. "Mr. Favia, how can we go about finding out where nursing homes are?"

The retired clown suggested that they go to the medical registry. He drove to the building and went inside with Nancy. They learned that there were two large and eight small nursing homes in the area.

As they went from one to another, Nancy asked if they had a patient by the name of either Lola Flanders or Laura Flynn. After they had inquired at six of them and received a negative reply, the three men became discouraged.

"We have four more to investigate," Nancy said cheerfully. "I'm not giving up yet!"

The last home they came to was a very shabby place. The house was in disrepair and badly in need of paint. Unlike others in the neighborhood, it had a weedy, run-down garden.

The men waited in the car while Nancy approached the house. The woman who answered her knock proved to be the owner. Her name was Mrs. Ayres and she was as shabby looking as her house. But in a moment, Nancy forgot all this.

In reply to Nancy's question, the woman said one of her patients was named Lola Flanders!

"I've come all the way from the United States to see her," said Nancy excitedly.

Mrs. Ayres stared at the visitor. "Well, it's too bad you went to all that trouble, miss," she said. "You can't see Lola Flanders. She has amnesia! She doesn't know who she is!"

CHAPTER XVII

The Hunt Narrows

Mrs. Ayres started to close the door of her nursing home.

"Oh, please!" Nancy said hurriedly. "I must talk to you."

The woman grudgingly invited Nancy to step inside and ushered her into a dark living room. The furnishings were threadbare and dilapidated.

"Would you mind telling me something about Mrs. Flanders?" Nancy asked, smiling disarmingly. "If she is the person I'm looking for, I know her daughter well. She is very anxious to find her mother."

Mrs. Ayres hesitated a moment, then said, "Lola Flanders is an American. She worked in a circus, where she had a bad fall. I don't know much about that. A man named Jones came here and asked me if I could board Lola. When I said I could, he brought her here. That's all I know."

"How long ago was this?" Nancy asked.

"Let me see," Mrs. Ayres said. "It must have been nearly ten years ago."

The date fitted the time when Lolita had been brought to America from Europe by the Kroons!

"Would you mind describing this Mr. Jones?" Nancy asked.

Mrs. Ayres' description fitted Reinhold Kroon. The pieces of the puzzle were falling together—fast!

"Did Lola Flanders bring any jewelry with her?" was Nancy's next question.

Mrs. Ayres looked startled. "Mr. Jones," she said haltingly, "is kind of slow paying. He never sends checks but shows up here once a year with the money. About three years ago he didn't come until very late. I couldn't keep Lola here for nothing—you know how it is," she said.

Nancy nodded and the woman went on with her story. Mrs. Ayres said that when she had talked to Lola about the situation, her patient had produced a very beautiful bracelet, which she had kept hidden in her luggage.

"Lola and I took a little trip to London to pawn it," Mrs. Ayres continued. "She didn't want to give her right name to the pawnbroker because she was kind of ashamed to have to pawn anything."

"So she used the name of Laura Flynn, didn't she?" Nancy asked.

Mrs. Ayres almost toppled from her chair in surprise. Nancy told her not to worry—that she had received the same bracelet as a gift and had been trying ever since to find out who the original owner had been.

"How long has Mrs. Flanders had amnesia?" she asked.

Mrs. Ayres replied that it was ever since Lola had come to live there. "She doesn't have complete amnesia," the woman said. "Every so often she seems to remember things very well. Then her memory will fade and for a long time she'll be almost like a child. To tell you the truth, Miss Drew, I think that medicine Lola takes has something to do with it."

"She's under a doctor's care?" Nancy asked.

Mrs. Ayres nodded and said that the physician was not a local man. He came once a month from London to see the ex-circus performer. He always left a supply of pills, which Lola was to take every day.

"You'll let me see Mrs. Flanders, won't you?" Nancy queried.

Once more, Mrs. Ayres seemed undecided as to what she should do. But finally she said, "I'm ready to wash my hands of the whole thing. It's very hard to keep Lola here on the small amount of money Mr. Jones gives me. Come on, I'll take you to her."

Nancy's pulse quickened as she followed the

woman up a narrow, winding stairway. Mrs. Ayres opened one of the bedroom doors and called out, "Lola, you have a visitor from the United States."

As Nancy walked in, she saw a small, sweet-looking woman seated in an old-fashioned rocker. There was no doubt in Nancy's mind that she was Lolita's mother!

"How do you do, Mrs. Flanders," she said, going forward and shaking hands with the woman. "I've come a long way to see you. How are you?"

"It's very nice to meet you, my dear," Mrs. Flanders said. "I never have any visitors."

Nancy told her that a former friend lived close by. He had seen her at a circus and had tried to speak to her. "But you left rather quickly," said Nancy.

Mrs. Flanders looked questioningly at Mrs. Ayres. Apparently she did not remember the incident.

"Oh yes, we went to the circus when it came here," said Mrs. Ayres. "Who is this person you speak of?"

"His name is Pietro Favia," Nancy said, watching Lolita's mother closely.

Mrs. Flanders jumped from her chair. For a few seconds her mind appeared clear. "Pietro!" she cried excitedly. "I remember him very well. He was one of the best clowns in the circus!"

Then suddenly the woman's face seemed to cloud over and she sat down in the rocker. "What were you asking me, my dear?" she said sweetly.

Mrs. Ayres shrugged as if to say to Nancy, "You see how it is." But the young detective was not discouraged. She felt that with proper care Lola's memory might be restored completely.

"I haven't told you," said Nancy, "but I'm a friend of your daughter Lolita."

"Lolita," Mrs. Flanders said softly. "My little Lolita died when she was very young."

Nancy was shocked. Apparently Mrs. Flanders had been told that her child was no longer living. Another of Kroon's tricks!

Nancy decided to change the subject. "Mrs. Flanders," she said, "a queen once gave you a beautiful bracelet with gold horse charms, didn't she?"

Again Lola Flanders rose from her chair and her eyes flashed. "Yes," she said excitedly. "Mrs. Ayres, where is my bracelet?"

Quickly pulling up her coat sleeve, Nancy asked, "Is this it?"

Mrs. Flanders stared at the bracelet as if she were seeing a ghost. Nancy took off the jewelry and put it around Mrs. Flander's thin wrist.

As the woman looked at it, all her uncertainty seemed to disappear. She smiled at Nancy and Mrs. Ayres.

"Please tell me more about this bracelet. How did you get it, Miss Drew?"

Nancy was brief. "It came from a shop in the

States," she said. "An aunt of mine saw it and bought it for me."

Nancy hurried on. Putting an arm about the woman, she said, "You think your daughter is no longer living. That isn't true. Lolita is alive and well. She lives in the United States."

"My little girl is alive!" Lola Flanders exclaimed happily.

Nancy nodded. "Would you like to see her?" she asked.

"Oh yes!" Mrs. Flanders said softly.

Nancy told her that Mr. Drew, who was a lawyer, was outside. He could make the legal arrangements for Lola Flanders to accompany them to the United States very soon. Nancy also revealed that Pietro Favia and his son were waiting with her father.

"Oh, I want to see them!" Lola Flanders cried.

Then suddenly she looked at her shabby clothes and shook her head. She said she could not possibly appear in public until she had her hair fixed and a new dress. Nancy and Mrs. Ayres laughed. For the next few minutes they helped Mrs. Flanders get ready. Nancy combed her hair into a more modern and becoming style. From a closet Mrs. Ayres brought out her own best dress. She wore it only to church, she said.

"Put this on," Mrs. Ayres suggested.

Lola Flanders slipped it over her head, and

"My little girl is alive!" Mrs. Flanders exclaimed.

smiling happily as a girl, surveyed herself in the mirror. When she was ready, the former circus performer went downstairs. Nancy hurried outside and brought in the men.

"Lola! Lola! This is wonderful!" the elder Pietro cried, kissing her.

Mrs. Flanders blushed. Then Nancy introduced her father and the younger Pietro.

"How soon could Mrs. Flanders be ready to leave?" Nancy asked Mrs. Ayres.

"Any time," the owner of the nursing home said. "She has very little in the way of luggage. It wouldn't take ten minutes to pack it."

Before Lola Flanders knew what was happening, she and her suitcase were in the big automobile, and she was saying good-by to Mrs. Ayres. The trip back to London did not take long.

Mr. Drew insisted that Mrs. Flanders be examined by another doctor. The physician revealed the patient had been under heavy medication and should be feeling her old self as soon as the drugs were out of her system.

By the following morning, Mr. Drew had made arrangements for taking Lola Flanders to the United States. He and Nancy had decided not to cable Lolita. While they hoped the flight would not tire Mrs. Flanders too much, they agreed that it would be better to wait until they arrived home before telling Lolita the wonderful news.

At the airport the two Pietros said good-by. The younger clown took Nancy aside. "Do you think I should tell Mrs. Flanders that Lolita and I are going to be married?" he asked.

"Not yet," Nancy advised. "Wait until she is feeling better."

The journey over the Atlantic was smooth and quick. When the plane landed in New York, a messenger was waiting with several telegrams. The stewardess came to Nancy's seat and handed one of them to her.

Quickly she tore it open, then stared at the paper in horror. The message had been sent from River Heights and read:

LOLITA BADLY INJURED. WILL MEET YOU HOTEL COLES NEW YORK WITH DETAILS.

                                        BESS

CHAPTER XVIII

Dodging Spies

For a moment Nancy sat in stunned silence. Then quickly she showed the telegram to her father, and in a whisper cautioned him not to read it aloud.

"Mrs. Flanders mustn't see it," she said hurriedly.

"You're right," her father agreed in a low voice. "This is dreadful news."

Trying not to show her agitation, Nancy helped Mrs. Flanders from the plane. The woman looked around in a daze. For a moment Nancy was afraid Mrs. Flanders might collapse from the strain of the trip. But suddenly the ex-circus performer smiled and said, "To think that I am back in the U. S. A.! Oh, it doesn't seem possible that in a little while I'll see my daughter again!"

"We'll have to find out where she is," said

Nancy gently. "I don't know where the circus is right now."

Mrs. Flanders was trembling with excitement. While Mr. Drew took their baggage through Customs, Nancy suggested that she sit down.

She led Mrs. Flanders to the women's lounge and asked the matron if she would please look after her for a few minutes. The kindly woman promised to do so.

"Please don't let her out of here," Nancy requested.

"Don't you worry, miss," the matron said. "I'll guard her as if she were my own relative."

Nancy hurried off to find her father. At the Customs desk, she said to him in a low voice, "Dad, I've just decided that the telegram is a hoax. Nobody in the States knew when we were flying back."

"It's just possible," said Mr. Drew, "that the doctor who attended Lola Flanders may have visited the nursing home and found out that she had left for the States. He could have cabled Kroon."

Nancy thought they should call Bess's home. Going at once to the telephone booth, she placed the call. Bess herself answered.

"Where are you?" she asked Nancy.

"New York City. I just landed. Bess, did you send me a telegram?"

"Why, no," Bess replied in surprise. "What made you think I had?"

Nancy told her that someone had signed her name to a very unfortunate message. Then she asked if Bess had heard from Lolita recently.

"Yes. I just spoke to Erika. Lolita is fine. Why do you want to know?"

Nancy told her about the latest developments. Bess gasped, first in horror that anyone could be so cruel as to send such a message, and then in delight to hear that Lolita's mother had been found.

"Where is the circus playing?" Nancy asked.

"It's moving to Melville tonight. They'll be there for three days. That's why Erika called me. She wanted to know about any news of Pietro."

Quickly Nancy gave Bess the details of the trip and concluded by saying that Pietro wanted to return to the circus as soon as possible and marry Lolita. "When Erika calls again, will you please give Lolita that message," she concluded.

Returning to her father, who had just received their baggage, Nancy told him the latest turn of events. Mr. Drew became grave.

"One thing is sure. We are being spied upon. We'll probably be followed. I suggest that we evade our pursuers and throw them off the track."

Nancy agreed. Suddenly an idea came to her. "I heard an announcement a few minutes ago that a helicopter's taking off for Newark. Suppose we fly over there and then drive back to New York? Anybody following us could never get there in time."

Mr. Drew smiled. "That's an excellent plan," he said to his daughter.

He went to buy the tickets while Nancy hurried to the women's lounge for Lola Flanders and then led her to the helicopter.

The trip to Newark and back was made in a little more than an hour. When they arrived at Eloise Drew's apartment, the lawyer took his sister aside to ask if Lola Flanders might stay at her apartment temporarily. Under the circumstances, it seemed best to keep her in hiding until they found out who had sent the strange telegram.

Eloise Drew was delighted with the arrangement. Nancy would stay with her also. Mr. Drew said he had to return to his office at once and would catch an afternoon plane to River Heights. After luncheon, Nancy said she would like to do an errand. Actually she wanted to talk to Captain Smith and tell him what she had found out in England. Miss Drew also said that she had an errand, which must be taken care of.

"Do you mind staying alone, Mrs. Flanders?" Nancy asked.

The woman laughed. It was the first time

Nancy had heard her laugh and it reassured the girl as to Lola Flanders' condition.

"Go ahead," Mrs. Flanders said. "You know, I feel like a new person. I have no more fears."

Nancy and her aunt left the apartment together. Miss Drew said she would not be gone more than twenty minutes, and Nancy could take all the time she needed. They separated, and Nancy went at once to call on Captain Smith.

"You back so soon? It's only been a few days." The officer shook his head. "Well, what's the news?"

After hearing Nancy's story, Captain Smith looked at her in admiration. He said no detective or police officer could have done a better job—and probably not so fast.

"There's still a lot to accomplish," Nancy said. "Have you found out any more about the Tristam Booking Agency or Lola Flanders' dividend checks?"

"I have some news that will amaze you," the officer said, "The Tristam Booking Agency has gone out of business!"

"It has?" Nancy asked in amazement.

The police officer said the firm had folded overnight and left no forwarding address.

"There has been no mail for Lola Flanders for two days," the captain stated. "I was just about to telephone one of the companies from which the dividend checks come to find out if they had been notified of a change of address. I'll do it now."

He put in a call to an oil company. Presently he received the information he wanted. Hanging up, he turned to Nancy and said, "Well, that's a break. The new address is the Hotel Coles in this city!"

Before Nancy could do any more than show her surprise, the captain was placing another call. This time it was to the hotel desk. He learned that a young dancer named Lola Flanders had registered there the day before.

Nancy told Captain Smith about the fake telegram, directing her to go to the Hotel Coles.

"But you didn't do it?" the man asked.

"No."

"I'm glad," the officer said. "It's in a bad neighborhood."

Captain Smith said he would send a detective to the hotel at once to check on Lola Flanders. He would have another man find out who had sent the telegram.

"Please call me at my aunt's home if you learn anything," Nancy requested.

The officer promised to do so and Nancy returned to the Drew apartment. She rang the bell and instantly the door was opened by her Aunt Eloise. She looked frightened.

"Nancy! Lola Flanders is gone!" she cried.

CHAPTER XIX

Terror at the Circus

"SHE must have had another attack of amnesia and wandered off!" Aunt Eloise said in despair.

"Or someone came here and persuaded her to leave," Nancy surmised.

Hastening to the street, Nancy asked some children playing there if they had seen a small sweet-faced woman leave the apartment house.

"I did," a little girl spoke up. "She and another lady got in a taxi."

"What did the other lady look like?" Nancy asked.

The little girl said the woman had curly blond hair and red cheeks. She had not heard them tell the driver where to go.

Nancy hurried upstairs and called Captain Smith. At her request he agreed to check the Hotel Coles. A few minutes later the officer called back to report that Millie Francine had not been at the hotel since she had registered.

An idea occurred to Nancy. Consulting the classified telephone directory, she made a series of calls to theater booking-agents and restaurants that employed dancers. The list was long and it was over an hour before she had any success. Then she found that Millie Francine was employed at the Bon Ton Night Club.

Nancy decided to get in touch with the dancer. Even if she knew nothing about Lolita's mother and her possible kidnapping, she might be able to give Nancy a lead to the guilty party.

As Nancy was wondering how to contact Millie, the doorbell rang. She ran to the door, hopeful that Lola Flanders had returned. Instead, Ned Nickerson stood there, a broad grin on his face.

"I know you didn't expect to see me," he said, stepping into the apartment. "I telephoned earlier to see if by any chance you were back. When I heard you were here, I came over!"

Nancy stared at him in surprise. "Who answered the phone when you called?"

"I don't know." Ned went on to tell Nancy that whoever had answered the phone had said that Nancy and Miss Drew were out and that she herself was just about to leave.

"Then she mumbled something about going to see her daughter," Ned remarked.

"Oh Ned," said Nancy, "it's just what I feared. Lola Flanders has been kidnapped!"

"What do you mean?"

Nancy told him the whole story and then said, "Ned, you and I are going to the Bon Ton as fast as we can get there."

"Well, I'm glad I have a date," Ned said, "but why pick out a place like that? Anyway, it won't be open in the afternoon."

Nancy looked discouraged. Then she said hopefully, "Maybe the girls in the act rehearse in the afternoon. Let's go anyway."

To Nancy's delight, the Bon Ton was open. As she had hoped, a rehearsal was going on. She and Ned sat down at a table in a dim corner and watched.

It was not difficult to identify Millie Francine because presently the director called out, "Millie, what's the matter with you? Your voice sounds as if you'd been eating gravel!"

Millie Francine seemed to be nervous. When her part in the show was over she sat down at a table not far from where Nancy and Ned were. They got up and went over to sit with her.

Nancy spoke in a low tone. "Where have you hidden the real Lola Flanders?"

Millie Francine fell back as if someone had struck her. In a quavering voice she asked Nancy who she was.

"I'm a detective and I know all about you,"

Nancy replied. She gave the girl enough of the story to convince her.

Shaking with fright, Millie declared she was innocent. "I used to be with Sims' Circus," she said. "Mr. Kroon knew I needed money. When he suggested I could earn some extra cash just by pretending my name was Lola Flanders, I didn't see any harm in doing it."

The dancer said she had been paid well by Kroon and Mr. Tristam, the owner of the agency.

"What about the mail that came to you in care of the agency?" Nancy asked.

Millie looked surprised. She said she had never received any mail there. Nancy told her about the dividend checks and her suspicion that Kroon and possibly Tristam were stealing them.

The dancer began to weep. She insisted that she had done nothing wrong and did not want to go to jail.

"I don't think you'll have to go to jail," said Nancy, "providing your story is true. It will help a lot if you tell us where Lola Flanders is right now."

"I don't know," said Millie. "The agency busted up, you know."

Nancy asked if Millie knew where the Tristams lived. She gave them an apartment house address.

"How soon will the rehearsal be over?" Nancy asked the dancer abruptly.

"I'm through now," the girl replied.

"In that case, I'll go to your dressing room and wait while you change. Then you're going with us to the apartment." Nancy was fearful the dancer might telephone the Tristams and spoil everything.

Millie Francine demurred.

"The easiest way to prove you're innocent," said Nancy, "is to face those people."

"I never thought of that," the dancer said. She led Nancy to her dressing room.

Twenty minutes later the three set off in a cab. Unbeknown to Nancy, Ned had telephoned Captain Smith and asked that a policeman meet them at the apartment house. Upon their arrival, they found him waiting.

Nancy suggested that Millie Francine call up to the apartment that she was there, but not to mention that she had other visitors with her. The dancer did her part and the front door was opened.

They rode up in the elevator to the third floor and found the Tristam apartment. Millie rang the bell. The door was opened by a woman with curly blond hair whom the dancer called Mrs. Tristam. The four callers burst in.

While the policeman stood guard at the door, Nancy and Ned hurried inside to look for Lola Flanders. They found her in the living room, talking to Mr. Tristam.

"Oh, Nancy!" Lolita's mother cried out. "It

was dreadful of me not to have left a note for you. These kind people got in touch with me and we were going to leave in a few minutes to see my daughter."

"Mrs. Flanders," said Nancy, "these people are not kind. They have practically kidnapped you, and have been stealing your money for years. They never intended to take you to Lolita."

As Lola Flanders fell back, stunned, Mr. Tristam walked forward. He demanded to know what this outrageous story was all about and who Nancy was.

"I'm quite sure you know who I am," she said. "Possibly you do not know my friend, Ned Nickerson. And in case you do not know the policeman at the door, I suggest that you meet him quietly."

Suddenly Tristam's eyes blazed and he became virtually a madman. He shoved Nancy aside and punched Ned. Then he started for the door to the hall. Before he could reach the policeman, Millie Francine planted herself in his path.

"Oh, no you don't, Mr. Tristam," she cried. "You don't go another step without telling these people I'm innocent!"

At that moment there was a tap on the door. The policeman recognized it as a signal from more of Captain Smith's men. He opened the door. The officer and two other men walked in.

Tristam surrendered. He told the story much

as Nancy had pieced it together. He added that it was all Kroon's idea. "When Lola Flanders, then a widow, was discharged from the hospital, he planned to keep her drugged so she would appear to be an amnesia victim. He placed her in a cheap nursing home. It was Mrs. Kroon who abducted Lolita, partly because she loved the little girl and partly because she knew the child had great talent and would bring a small fortune to them."

Nancy was fearful that the excitement might upset Lola Flanders, but she seemed to have recovered completely. When they reached Aunt Eloise's apartment, Mrs. Flanders asked how soon they would start for Melville to see Lolita.

"If you feel well enough, we'll take the first plane," Nancy promised her.

"I'm ready to go now," she insisted.

Ned obtained the reservations and within two hours they were all saying good-by to Aunt Eloise and setting off for the town of Melville.

As they climbed into the plane, the first person they saw was young Pietro! He explained that he had just arrived from England.

"I couldn't stay away," he said. "Nancy, I had a hunch you would solve everything and that it won't be long before Lolita and I can be married."

"I think you're right," Nancy said, smiling at Ned, "and Lolita will have her wish—that her mother will be present at the wedding."

The plane reached Melville just before midnight. The group went to the hotel. Nancy suggested that Lola Flanders remain there until Lolita could be brought to her.

"I don't know whether Mr. Kroon has been apprehended yet or not," Nancy said. Turning to Ned and Pietro, she added, "Suppose we three go over to the circus at five o'clock tomorrow morning and mingle with the crowd watching the workmen set up the tents. Then we won't be noticed by Mr. or Mrs. Kroon or any of their spies. We'll get Lolita and bring her back here."

The plan was agreed upon. Nancy was up at four thirty the next morning, and at five set off with the young men. Upon reaching the circus grounds, the three separated, Nancy going ahead. She made her way carefully to Lolita's trailer and knocked.

"Lolita, wake up!"

Sleepily the young aerialist tumbled out of bed and opened the door. Seeing Nancy, she started to cry out.

"Sh-h-h!" Nancy warned her. "Your real mother is in a hotel downtown. Get ready quietly and follow me."

Lolita dressed quickly and stepped out of her trailer.

"Oh, Nancy, this is marvelous! Let's hurry!" The two girls sped past the wild-animal cages to

avoid detection by Kroon, should he happen to
be around. But they did not see him and they ran
on happily.

They had just reached King Kat's cage when a
strong hand was suddenly laid on Nancy's shoulder. The person gripped her tightly and swung
her about.

Kroon!

"So you're still trying to thwart me!" the man
cried. "Well, this is the last time!"

With his free hand, he unfastened the lion's
cage and thrust Nancy forward!

CHAPTER XX

Last Links in the Mystery

WITH a great leap the huge lion sprang toward the door of the cage. Nancy Drew fought to get away from the insane ringmaster, who was pushing her into the cage. Lolita screamed and tried to pull her foster father away.

A few yards behind Nancy was Ned Nickerson. And a short distance behind him, Pietro. Both young men raced forward with lightning speed.

Ned grasped Nancy and swung her away from the lion. The angry, confused beast landed one claw on the boy's hand and raked it badly.

Ned's action had startled Kroon, who fell backward. The lion hesitated a moment as though undecided as to whether to slink away or jump forward. For a fearful second everyone wondered whether the beast would get loose.

Pietro saw a long whip lying on the ground.

Quickly he picked it up and cracked the whip across King Kat's nose. The lion snarled and bared its teeth. One paw, halfway through the opening, was keeping Pietro from closing the cage door. With another crack of the whip he struck the lion's paw and the beast jumped backward with a roar of pain. The clown slammed and locked the door.

By this time there was pandemonium in the circus. Every workman and many of the performers had come on the run to see what had happened. In the melee, Kroon disappeared.

"Oh, Nancy!" Lolita cried. "Are you all right?"

Nancy nodded. Recovering from her shock, she saw that Ned's hand was bleeding profusely.

"Ned!" she said quickly. "You must go to Dr. Jackson at once!" Then, realizing that she had not thanked him for rescuing her, she added, "Ned, you saved my life!"

Ned smiled. "Nancy, I'm thankful I was here to do it. And these scratches aren't bad."

Pietro, too, was thanked.

Quickly Nancy looked around. "Where did Mr. Kroon go?" she asked.

No one had noticed him leave. Nancy, determined to prevent his escape, asked Lolita to take Ned to the doctor.

"Pietro," she said, "we must find Mr. Kroon."

The man was not on the circus grounds, and Mrs. Kroon also was missing. Pietro reported that the ringmaster's car was gone. Nancy telephoned State Police headquarters and spoke to the sergeant on duty. She was told that the police had just received word from New York to apprehend Kroon and were about to pick him up at the circus.

"Thank you, Miss Drew," the sergeant said. "I'll send a detail out at once and we'll set up a road block."

The Kroons were picked up a short time later on the highway and taken to headquarters. Nancy, Lolita, Pietro, and Ned were present at the interrogation.

Kroon, finding that denials of his crooked schemes were futile and that even his two spies, the tramp clown and the giant, had not been entirely loyal to him, made a full confession. He did not spare the Tristams, on whom he put a great deal of the blame.

At Kroon's request, Tristam had come to River Heights and stolen the horse-charm bracelet. He had brought it to Kroon, who years before had had a cheap duplicate of Lolita's horse charm made. He had kept the original, hoping to obtain the valuable bracelet, and had finally succeeded.

But when Nancy had stymied his plan to sell it, Kroon and Tristam together had engineered the kidnapping of Nancy and George. Learning that this had failed, Tristam had found out where Nancy had gone and followed her to New York. He had tried to stop Nancy's trip to England by engaging a professional gangster to put the acid in her overnight bag.

While Kroon and Tristam had managed to steal the dividend checks that had come to Lola Flanders from her securities, they had never dared to try selling the securities themselves. Lolita was thrilled to hear that they were still intact for her mother.

When Kroon finished his confession, the police asked Nancy and the others if they had any questions. The girl detective spoke up.

"I have just one," she said. "Mr. Kroon, who was it that went to the riding academy and attacked Señor Roberto?"

The ringmaster said Tristam had done this also. Both he and Kroon felt that Hitch was in the way. Tristam had meant to attack the stableman, but had, in the semidarkness, mistaken Roberto for him. Just as he had discovered his error, Tristam heard voices in the distance and fled.

After all the angles of the mystery were cleared up, Nancy and her friends went at once to the Melville Hotel. Nancy suggested that no one attend the reunion of mother and daughter. Lolita

smiled and thanked Nancy for being so understanding, but said that she wanted all of the others
to come to her mother's room in an hour.

When Nancy and the young men arrived, they
were thrilled to see the happiness on the faces of
Lola and Lolita Flanders. Their praise of Nancy
was boundless, and Ned and Pietro were heartily
thanked also.

"Mother and I have been talking over my wedding plans," said Lolita, blushing a little. "Mother
has a wonderful idea."

The others listened eagerly as the pretty aerialist went on to say that Mrs. Flanders would like
the wedding to take place soon—three days from
then.

"This is partly because she wants her daughter
and her new son-in-law in business with her," Lolita explained.

Pietro looked puzzled. "In business?" he asked.

"Yes," said Lola Flanders, taking hold of the
young clown's hand. "I had a telephone call a
little while ago from Nancy's Aunt Eloise. The
New York police have discovered that Sims' Circus is a stock company and I own most of the
stock."

"That's wonderful!" Nancy cried out, delighted.

Pietro asked how Sims figured in the deal.
Lola Flanders told him that at one period, when

the circus was about to fold up, Lolita's father had bought the major portion of the stock. Kroon knew this and kept reminding young Mr. Sims of the fact whenever he stayed around the circus too long.

The ringmaster had confidentially told him that it was still a mystery as to whether Lola Flanders was alive. Someday she might show up and claim her rightful share. Since young Sims knew little about running a circus, he had gladly left this to the stronger-willed Kroon.

Pietro suddenly kissed his future mother-in-law. Then he said, "Bad as Mr. Kroon was, I certainly have him to thank for one thing. Sims is still a fine circus."

"Indeed it is," said Lolita. "Mother, wait until you see a performance."

Nancy asked what had happened to the Vascon troupe. Lolita said that when Rosa had been unable to perform, Mr. Kroon had discharged the whole equestrian troupe. Suddenly Lolita looked at Nancy.

"Oh," she said, "it would be so wonderful if they would come back and we could have a full performance on the night of the wedding. Nancy, would you ride in Rosa's place?"

The girl detective smiled and said she would be very happy to take part in the act.

The night of the gala performance Nancy's

family and friends sat in Box AA, with Señor Roberto, who had fully recovered from his injuries.

Bess whispered to George, "This is so marvelous I could cry. It's the best mystery Nancy ever solved."

"It was swell," George agreed. "But you just wait. Another good mystery will come Nancy's way and I'll bet it won't be long, either."

George was right! Nancy had hardly recovered from her days at the circus when she was confronted with *The Scarlet Slipper Mystery*.

During the gala evening, it seemed as though each performer outdid himself. Nancy felt as if she had never done her stunt riding so well. The wedding plans had been announced to the audience, and after the finale, everyone stayed in his seat.

The happy bride and her real prince were married in the great circus ring. Then, as they walked out together, smiling, and the band played, the applause was thunderous.

A reception had been arranged in the cafeteria tent. The wedding gifts were displayed in one corner on a large table. Prominent among them was the picture of Nancy Drew, standing on a horse in her circus costume. Lola Flanders had asked Eloise Drew for it.

A little later the radiant bride said to Nancy,

"This will be a constant reminder of the most wonderful girl I have ever met!"

Then Lolita held up her arm on which she was wearing the beautiful horse-charm bracelet.

"Are you sure you want me to have this as a wedding gift?" she asked Nancy.

"Of course I do," Nancy replied. "The bracelet came from a queen and now it has come back to one—the queen of aerialists!"

ORDER FORM

NANCY DREW
MYSTERY SERIES

by Carolyn Keene

55 TITLES AT YOUR BOOKSELLER OR
COMPLETE THIS HANDY COUPON AND MAIL TO:

GROSSET & DUNLAP, INC.
P.O. Box 941, Madison Square Post Office, New York, N.Y. 10010

Please send me the Nancy Drew Mystery Book(s) checked below @ $2.95 each, plus 25¢ per book postage and handling. My check or money order for $_____ is enclosed. (Please do not send cash.)

☐	1.	Secret of the Old Clock	9501-7	☐ 28.	The Clue of the Black Keys	9528-9
☐	2.	Hidden Staircase	9502-5	☐ 29.	Mystery at the Ski Jump	9529-7
☐	3.	Bungalow Mystery	9503-3	☐ 30.	Clue of the Velvet Mask	9530-0
☐	4.	Mystery at Lilac Inn	9504-1	☐ 31.	Ringmaster's Secret	9531-9
☐	5.	Secret of Shadow Ranch	9505-X	☐ 32.	Scarlet Slipper Mystery	9532-7
☐	6.	Secret of Red Gate Farm	9506-8	☐ 33.	Witch Tree Symbol	9533-5
☐	7.	Clue in the Diary	9507-6	☐ 34.	Hidden Window Mystery	9534-3
☐	8.	Nancy's Mysterious Letter	9508-4	☐ 35.	Haunted Showboat	9535-1
☐	9.	The Sign of the Twisted Candles	9509-2	☐ 36.	Secret of the Golden Pavilion	9536-X
☐	10.	Password to Larkspur Lane	9510-6	☐ 37.	Clue in the Old Stagecoach	9537-8
☐	11.	Clue of the Broken Locket	9511-4	☐ 38.	Mystery of the Fire Dragon	9538-6
☐	12.	The Message in the Hollow Oak	9512-2	☐ 39.	Clue of the Dancing Puppet	9539-4
☐	13.	Mystery of the Ivory Charm	9513-0	☐ 40.	Moonstone Castle Mystery	9540-8
☐	14.	The Whispering Statue	9514-9	☐ 41.	Clue of the Whistling Bagpipes	9541-6
☐	15.	Haunted Bridge	9515-7	☐ 42.	Phantom of Pine Hill	9542-4
☐	16.	Clue of the Tapping Heels	9516-5	☐ 43.	Mystery of the 99 Steps	9543-2
☐	17.	Mystery of the Brass Bound Trunk	9517-3	☐ 44.	Clue in the Crossword Cipher	9544-0
				☐ 45.	Spider Sapphire Mystery	9545-9
☐	18.	Mystery at Moss-Covered Mansion	9518-1	☐ 46.	The Invisible Intruder	9546-7
				☐ 47.	The Mysterious Mannequin	9547-5
☐	19.	Quest of the Missing Map	9519-X	☐ 48.	The Crooked Banister	9548-3
☐	20.	Clue in the Jewel Box	9520-3	☐ 49.	The Secret of Mirror Bay	9549-1
☐	21.	The Secret in the Old Attic	9521-1	☐ 50.	The Double Jinx Mystery	9550-5
☐	22.	Clue in the Crumbling Wall	9522-X	☐ 51.	Mystery of the Glowing Eye	9551-3
☐	23.	Mystery of the Tolling Bell	9523-8	☐ 52.	The Secret of the Forgotten City	9552-1
☐	24.	Clue in the Old Album	9524-6			
☐	25.	Ghost of Blackwood Hall	9525-4	☐ 53.	The Sky Phantom	9553-X
☐	26.	Clue of the Leaning Chimney	9526-2	☐ 54.	The Strange Message In the Parchment	9554-8
☐	27.	Secret of the Wooden Lady	9527-0	☐ 55	Mystery of Crocodile Island	9555-6

SHIP TO:

NAME _____
(please print)

ADDRESS _____

CITY _____ STATE _____ ZIP _____

Please do not send cash.